PRAISE FOR

FINDING [barcode: P9-EDV-598]

"Bianca is an extremely likeable character: smart, funny, and able to find humor in the worst situations. The author does a great job of capturing her voice. An entertaining read."

—*School Library Journal*

"This lively and captivating mystery is even more fun than the first."

—*VOYA* (Voice of Youth Advocates)

"Simply a delight... Bianca is one of the funniest characters to come out of young adult fiction in years."

—*Mystery Morgue*

UNCOVERING SADIE'S SECRETS

"Extra entertainment for mystery fans, one for those who want a puzzle without a ghost or murder."

—*Kirkus Reviews*

"A lightweight, lively, and entertaining teen mystery-romance. Nancy Drew fans and other young mystery aficionados will be pleased."

—*Booklist*

"A great start to what looks like a continuing series."

—*School Library Journal*

"An engaging young teen mystery... A fine present for the female Harry Potter crowd."

—*Harriet's Book Reviews*

"This lightweight and enjoyable mystery will be especially appreciated by female readers and is appropriate for school and public libraries."

—*VOYA* (Voice of Youth Advocates)

DANGEROUS LIAISONS

"May I have the honor of escorting you, mademoiselle?" Neville asked.

Remembering my Honors French, I said, "Mais oui, monsieur," which is about all I could manage without sounding like I had a mouth full of marbles. It must have been enough, though, because he took my hand and looped it over his arm, bending his head toward me as if we shared a secret.

"Don't look now, m'dear, but I think the guard is eyeing you rather suspiciously. You didn't, by any chance, slip a painting into your brassiere?" Then he looked at me with a wolflike gaze that made me tremble and blush. "But of course you couldn't. Not the way that dress hugs you so deliciously."

I don't think I've ever been described as "delicious" before. And if some guy at school had just said that to me, I'd have swung at him. Or at least squinted. But somehow Neville could get away with saying a whole lot of things just because of his dreamy British accent. So when he pulled me a little closer, I didn't resist, and that's exactly how my boyfriend found us. Oops.

FINDING the FORGER

LIBBY STERNBERG

SMOOCH NEW YORK CITY

To Mary Ann...down by the seashore, sifting sand.

SMOOCH ®

March 2006

Published by

Dorchester Publishing Co., Inc.
200 Madison Avenue
New York, NY 10016

ISBN 0-8439-5503-1

The name "SMOOCH" and its logo are trademarks of Dorchester Publishing Co., Inc.

Printed in the United States of America.

Visit us on the web at www.smoochya.com.

FINDING the FORGER

Chapter One

Did you know you can sing the words of "Amazing Grace" to the tune of the "Gilligan's Island" theme song? Try it. I'll wait.

The "Amazing Grace" trick is one of the things I learned recently in Mr. Baker's music class at St. John's High School, where I, Bianca Balducci, am a sophomore.

Mr. Baker is small and balding. Because of that, and his quick, darting movements, he reminds me of a bird. A bird with a bow tie. He has about a kajillion bow ties—in red, plaid, green (for St. Patrick's Day), polka-dot, blue, and even one that lights up and plays "Silent Night" for Christmas. I bet he wears a bow tie to bed.

Anyway, Baker had to take over from Mrs. Williston in early November, right after we did "The Mikado," because Williston, without her glasses on, took an on-stage bow, and tumbled into the orchestra pit, breaking her leg. Hey—don't look at me. I was nowhere near her!

Baker usually comes in part-time only to accompany rehearsals, but with Williston out, he was brought on full-time. He taught us the "Amazing Grace" trick to illustrate what hymn "meter" is and how in the back of hymnals, the tunes are usually arranged by meter as well as by title, so you can switch words with different tunes.

When he finished his explanation and we all giggled our way through "Amazing Grace" sung to the Gilligan theme, he pursed his lips together and said, "Now, I know that in your *Roman* tradition, you don't sing many metered *hymns*, but it's an important part of an understanding of *music*, particularly religious music outside of the *Latin* milieu."

That's when it dawned on me. Since Baker is an organist at one of Baltimore's Episcopalian churches, he probably figured all of us St. John's students were Catholics (*Roman* Catholics) and that we chanted away the hours in Latin at the crack of a nun's ruler on our knuckles.

Talk about false assumptions. In reality, only about three nuns work at St. John's, and one's the principal. And about half (or more) of the student body probably checked "other" on the part of the entrance app that asks whether you're a Catholic. Poor old Mr. Baker was working with outdated stereotypes of parochial schools and the "Roman" faith in general. But we don't disabuse him of his myths. We think it's kind of cute the way he calls all the women teachers "Sister."

And that brings me to this story, which is really about false assumptions and how my friend Sarah's crush almost landed in jail, how my other best friend, Kerrie, almost ended up hating me, and how I almost ended up without a boyfriend just after I'd landed one.

But I'm getting ahead of myself.

It was the Monday right after Thanksgiving and I was sitting on a hard, cold bench outside the City Art Museum waiting with my friend Sarah. Sarah, a senior, who first came to our school calling herself Sadie, was doing an after-school internship at the museum, and she'd asked me to go with her that day so we could plan a surprise birthday party for our mutual friend Kerrie. Since we arrived fifteen minutes before her internship began and she had to go in, we were snarfing a quick snack and "planning."

I was in a glum mood after a crappy day. In fact, my mood matched the weather—gray, overcast, and ready to spit something. Not only had Mr. Baker singled me out for ridicule during chorus ("Miss Balducci, is that the alto line you're singing or a frog croaking?"), but Kerrie and Sarah had squabbled at lunch like parents in a bad custody case. And I had been in the middle. Oh, it hadn't been an out-and-out fight. That's boy stuff. It was one of those subtle girl spats where you need a United Nations translator murmuring in the background to tell you what's really being said. Example:

Me (*as Kerrie plops her books on cafeteria table at lunch*): What's the matter?

Kerrie (*shrugging*): Nothing. (*Translation: everything*)

Sarah: Are we getting together this afternoon, Bianca? (*Translation: you're not doing anything with Kerrie, are you?*)

Kerrie: Hey, Bianca, I thought you and I were getting together so I could show you what to do with your hair for the dance. (*Translation: so you've betrayed me again, have you?*)

Sarah: She has to go over some math with me (*Translation: tongue sticking out*)

Kerrie: That's crazy—Bianca doesn't need help in math. Right, Bianc? (*Translation: choose wisely, girl*)

So you can see why I was in a crappy mood. Oh, and did I forget to mention that my boyfriend, Doug, had walked by after lunch to ask if I wanted to get together after school? And I had to say I couldn't because I was being pulled in two directions by two girlfriends, and getting together with them was going to be so much more fun than spending time with him?

Speaking of fun, do you see the irony here? Sarah was bickering with Kerrie about spending time with me so she could plan a surprise birthday party for the afore-mentioned Kerrie. No wonder guys have such a hard time understanding girls. I'm a girl and I don't understand them!

The museum was closed to visitors on Mondays, so the place was shut up tight and quiet as a tomb.

"The problem is going to be getting Kerrie out of the house while we get ready," Sarah said, grabbing another cookie from the cellophane wrapper. She hugged her navy blue blazer closer. Even though Baltimore usually doesn't get super cold in December, the air was damp and chilly, and clouds kept the sun from warming our shoulders. Everything was as colorless as the museum's stone walls.

I chewed on a Fig Newton and said nothing.

Sarah lives with Kerrie's family. She'd been living with them for about a month, in fact, ever since Kerrie's dad, a lawyer, helped Sarah out of a big mess. While Kerrie had thought it a grand idea at the time, she soon discov-ered that having a live-in sibling wasn't just an eternal sleepover, with hours of gossip and sharing and giggling fun. It was more like a purgatory of minor annoyances. I know. I have two siblings—my sister Connie (who's a pri-vate investigator) and my brother Tony (who's a college student).

One of the points of tension between Kerrie and Sarah was the fact that Kerrie was no longer the center of attention in her household. In fact, Sarah was pretty high-maintenance right now. She had been spending vir-

4

tually every weekend looking at colleges with Mr. and Mrs. Daniels. And because Sarah was smack up against deadlines, they were helping her with her college apps, too, which didn't leave a lot of time left over for Kerrie.

"Listen," Sarah continued, "you're not coming up with suggestions—how will we get Kerrie to the party and keep it a surprise?"

"I could invite her over to my house," I volunteered. "She could do my hair!" I looked at my watch. Speaking of hair, I was going to have to hurry if I wanted to be on time at Kerrie's for today's hair appointment. And I suspected Kerrie would be annoyed if I was late.

Sarah shrugged. "What if she won't go? You know how she sometimes turns an invite out into one over to the house?" Sarah still wasn't used to thinking of the Daniels family as her family, even in a temporary sense. So she always referred to their home as "the home" or "the house"—never "my home," or "our house."

"She's interested in Russell Cooper, isn't she? Maybe I can say he's there or something."

"Bianca, how in the world would you get Russell Cooper to your house? Does Doug know him?"

"Well, only a little." Russell and Doug moved in different circles. While Doug was an average guy, Russell was on the debate team, taking AP Physics, AP Calculus, *and* AP English, and applying to Harvard and Yale next year. "But he's a guy. Guys can ask guys to do things that girls can't."

Sarah let out an exasperated sigh. "That's not the only problem. Getting the food and stuff in without Kerrie's seeing is going to be a major hassle. And the invites and the music—I thought it would be neat to find any song we could with 'sixteen' in it and play it."

"That would really embarrass her," I said. "Good idea."

Embarrassing your friends is, after all, a symbol of your deep affection for them.

"You need to do the invite list," Sarah added. "I don't have a handle on all her friends."

"Okay," I said, cringing. Putting together the invitation list would be a bear. Our school had a rule—no invitations given out at school unless the whole class is getting one. That meant I'd have to actually find addresses for people and send cards to their homes.

Hmmm . . . maybe this was something Doug and I could do together. Images of a cozy afternoon sitting at my kitchen table, hot chocolate in hand, music on the CD, family members secured in closets so they wouldn't embarrass us, ran through my head. Could be fun. "I'd love to do it!" I finally said.

"The biggest challenge is going to be finding a day to do this," Sarah said, crumpling the now-empty cellophane wrapper in her hand. She strode to a nearby trash bin and tossed the paper in. "Every time I suggest doing something lately, Kerrie backs off."

"Yeah, I know."

"She's doing it to you, too?"

"Well, not exactly." Actually, not at all. I sensed Sarah was nudging up to a heart-to-heart about Kerrie, which made me a little uncomfortable. Then again, the last time I'd turned a deaf ear to a friend's problem had almost ended disastrously, so I stepped up to the plate and dived in, to mix metaphors. "I think she's just a little grumpy because things aren't the way they used to be."

"But she was the one who insisted I stay with them!" Sarah straightened and stared into the distance. Sitting on her hands, she turned to me, her eyes shining with the unshed tears of the falsely accused. "She had to convince *me*!"

"Life is funny, isn't it?" I said. Would I make a great counselor or what?

("Failing every grade?" No problem, I'd advise—life is funny.)

("Parents getting divorced?" No sweat—life is funny.)

Squaring my shoulders, I continued. "I mean, I have a feeling Kerrie didn't really know what she wanted. And now . . ." Way to go, Bianca. How to finish that phrase—"And now, Sarah, she's stuck with you."

"What I mean," I said after clearing my throat, "is Kerrie probably didn't realize that sharing her home with a friend actually means sharing. She probably expected everything to stay the way it was. For example, the computer." I was getting into this. Feeling like a schoolteacher, I stood in front of Sarah. "The computer used to be just Kerrie's—in her room for her personal use. Mr. Daniels had his own computer in his study. Now where's Kerrie's computer?" I knew the answer to this, but when teaching, it's important for the student to say the answer out loud.

"In a corner of the dining room."

"Right. So you *both* can use it for homework. And what about the TV?"

"Well, there's a TV in the living room and one in Kerrie's room."

"And Kerrie has to share it with you, right?"

"Right, but I hardly ever ask to watch anything special. The only times I watch in there are when she invites me to watch something with her." Sarah looked frustrated and annoyed, curling the strap of her backpack around her finger over and over again. She looked at her watch, and I knew she was thinking of going into work early just to get away from this uncomfortable discussion, so I sped up.

7

"Exactly. She's asking you to watch with her because she feels it's the right thing to do, but she's probably remembering those glorious days when she was Empress of the Remote all by herself and didn't need to think of anyone else's feelings."

"Well, if that's all it is, I can use the computers at school, and I just won't watch TV with her at all," Sarah said with a "harrumph" in her voice.

That wasn't all there was, though, but I didn't feel comfortable delving into the deep recesses of a kid's relationship with her parents. Kerrie probably didn't like sharing attention with her folks, especially her father, whom she adored. It was one thing for Kerrie to give up TV and computer privileges for the sake of family harmony, but quite another for her to sacrifice a parental relationship when she really needed one. Besides, Sarah would be off at college in less than a year and Kerrie would be back in single-child heaven. As much as I loved Kerrie, I thought she needed to do a little more giving in this regard.

To get away from this uncomfortable topic, I changed the subject.

"How's the internship going?" I asked, nodding toward the hulking museum.

She shrugged. "It's okay. But there's some weird stuff going on. Like my boss—Fawn Dexter—is on the phone a lot."

"So?"

"So she closes the door whenever she sees me or somebody else coming. And she talks low, in a whisper, like she doesn't want us to hear."

"Maybe it's confidential museum stuff."

"No, I think it's something personal. I can hear her laughing and kind of flirting, if you know what I mean."

Ah yes—the old flirt voice, recognizable to any woman over the age of twelve. That little hush, that mellow giggle, that smooth whisper. So what if Sarah's boss was using it?

Speaking of the flirt voice, that's exactly what Sarah used when a stranger started approaching us. Dressed in tan slacks and dark blazer, he was dark-skinned, dark-haired, and pretty darn good-looking. When Sarah saw him, she stood and smoothed her uniform skirt the way you do when you want to make sure you look your best. Not that her skirt needed smoothing. She was like a bird preening. I got the picture. She liked this fellow.

"Hector!" she called out in this throaty, come-hither tone. "I was just getting ready to start work."

"Me, too," he said, joining us.

"Bianca, this is Hector Gonzalez. He goes to UMBC and works part-time here as a security guard." Sarah turned to me. "Hector, this is Bianca Balducci, my friend. We go to school together."

"I gathered," he said, looking at our uniforms and smiling. He had a nice warm smile that showed off even teeth. "Come on, you're going to be late. Don't want to create a bad impression."

"Hey, my brother goes to UMBC!" I said. "Economics major. Tony Balducci. Ever run into him?"

"Nope. But it's a big campus," Hector said, then reached out his arm and touched Sarah on the elbow as a signal it was time they got going.

Was it my imagination or was Sarah blushing? She looked down at her feet and picked up her backpack. I made a mental note to add Hector Gonzalez to the invitation list for Kerrie's party, which we'd probably schedule sometime after the first of the year.

As they say in those old novels, I made ready to leave.

9

But as I walked away, the quiet of the old museum was broken by several cars screeching into the little parking lot like they were just finishing a car race. Hector turned and looked at them, narrowing his eyes as he figured out who they were.

"Police," he said to Sarah. Then he checked a pager on his belt. "Silent alarm went off. You stay put. I'll see what's up."

As Hector walked away, Sarah looked at me kind of wild-eyed. "I might give Connie a call later, if that's okay," she said.

Chapter Two

Alarm at museum goes off and Sarah wants to talk to my PI sister Connie? Not good. The last time Sarah had wanted to talk to Connie was when Sarah was in deep doo-doo. Would she never learn?

"You can tell *me* whatever you want to tell Connie," I said. "We're practically partners." Well, this wasn't entirely true—I was still only on the short list for summer clerical help in Connie's PI office, but a girl can dream, right?

Sarah grimaced, looked at her watch, sighed heavily, and looked like she was going to clam up.

"C'mon," I urged. "Something's bugging you."

She swooped her hand toward the museum. "I told you. Something weird's going on. My boss has been talking to a private detective agency . . . about hiring them."

"What for?"

"I don't know!"

"Something else is bugging you. What is it?"

Sarah looked at the door Hector had gone through.

"I've overheard Fawn saying things about Hector."

"So?" Was I good at interrogating or what?

"Bad things, I think." Sarah chewed on her fingernail. "Like 'he's the only one who's been around each time' "

"Each time *what?*"

"I don't know!"

Before I could ask more questions, a door opened behind her and several police officers wandered out.

"I'll talk to you later," Sarah said, then disappeared into the building.

With that unsatisfying conversation bumping around in my head, I caught the bus on Charles Street for Kerrie's. By now, my irritation-meter was in the red zone. Sarah and I hadn't planned much of the party, so it was a mostly wasted half hour. She'd hinted at a museum mystery, but left important details out. And now I was headed to Kerrie's to give her equal time, when I had other, better things to do.

Things like Christmas shopping.

Specifically, I needed to get started on finding a gift for Doug. This would be our first Christmas as boyfriend/girlfriend, and the gift-giving scene is fraught with peril. Buy something too expensive and it looks like you're trying to ratchet up the relationship too fast. Buy something too small and it looks like you don't care enough. Plus, it's hard to buy for boys to begin with. It could take weeks of shopping to get the right thing. I was already behind schedule.

Speaking of shopping, the Dougster himself had told me after school he was headed to the mall with his mom tomorrow afternoon. That had sounded promising, and I had immediately imagined him looking at an expensive but significant piece of jewelry, or some rare perfume, or a watch, a silk scarf, a CD of love songs—and I hadn't even begun concocting a plan for dropping hints. But then he'd told me he "needed some new clothes" and my hopes hit the floor with a thunderous splat.

Luckily, I managed to snag a bus right away and landed on Kerrie's doorstep exactly two minutes before our appointed meeting time. Her mood was considerably lighter than it had been at school earlier, which I attributed to the fact that she had the house, and me, to herself.

Her house was in Fells Point, an area of town near the Harbor that was undergoing some urban renewal. Since her father was a lawyer and her mother a doctor, Kerrie's house always looked . . . well, like two well-compensated professionals paid the bills.

"I have a fantastic idea for your hair!" Kerrie shouted, brush in hand.

Warning bells should have gone off then and there. Since when does any good come from those words—"I have a fantastic idea for your hair"? But who was I to stand in the way of friendship? Kerrie needed coddling and my hair would have to do.

"I stopped by the drugstore on the way home," she said, leading me upstairs. "And I got something for you."

The "something" turned out to be a permanent wave kit. You see, Kerrie had done my hair in some wavy style for her Halloween party, when I'd come as a flapper (costume provided by her, of course). Normally, my hair is straight as a stick and just as boring, but she had managed, through the skillful use of pin-curls and hair-spray, to turn it into a waving, curling mass of seduction.

"I don't know, Ker," I said, looking at the box on her bed and removing my backpack. "That's a perm."

"No, it's not," she said huffily. She grabbed the box and read the label. "It's a hair curling and wave set."

"Same thing. Chemicals. Frizz. Smell."

"It says it has a green apple scent."

"Well, yeah, but what about the other stuff? The last time I had a perm was when I was seven and my mom took me to the beauty parlor that my Aunt Rosa's sister-in-law owns. Mom wanted me to get a cut for my First Communion, but they convinced her to let me have a perm."

"And?"

"And . . . have I ever shown you pictures taken at my First Communion?"

"No."

"Well, there you have it. We destroyed them all so no one could blackmail me when I was older."

"Aw, c'mon, Bianca. That was probably some Old World kind of thing. They have new kits now that aren't nearly as strong."

("Old World perm"? Was that the kind immigrants brought with them to the "new perm" country?)

"Look," Kerrie added. "We'll do a little test and if you don't like the result, we won't go ahead."

I took a look at the smiling model on the box, her coiled locks as inviting as the Sirens' songs, remembered how Doug had looked at me when he saw me in my festive 'do, and decided, what the heck? If the test failed, we'd cancel the procedure, right?

Do I even need to tell you how this all turned out? Aren't you filling in the blanks yourself about now?

Okay, okay, here are your choices:

a) the perm test frizzed Bianca's hair, thus warning her not to proceed;

b) the perm test curled some hairs and frizzed others, and another test was conducted;

c) the perm test went fine because the whole concoction was a wicked prank the manufacturers devised to sucker unsuspecting beauty wannabes into their cackling clutches.

If you chose "c," you've entered the dark recesses of a heart broken by bad hair.

No, my friends, "bad hair" doesn't begin to describe this experience. It doesn't even come close.

At the end of an hour and a half of chemicals soaking into my head—chemicals that smelled like green apples all right, just green apples left to ripen for a month in a well-used litter box—after having my hair pulled and squeezed and tangled around little plastic rollers whose rubber band closures were modeled after tools used by the monks of the Inquisition, after looking at Kerrie's troubled face and saying "what's that burning smell?" only to realize it was the odor of my hair being singed by the strong "new world" perm compounds—after all this, my friends, I had the pleasure of looking in the mirror and realizing my life as a girlfriend had come to a screeching halt. I had the tire tracks on my head to prove it.

Think white girl Afro. Think Annie. Think Brillo.

My permed hair stood out from my head almost a foot in every direction, except for one lock on the side that dangled straight out. That was the test lock.

"I'm sure it will loosen up overnight," Kerrie said uncomfortably as I stared in the mirror, trying hard not to put my hands around her neck and throttle her. Why, oh why, did I let her talk me into this? So what if she had been feeling a little mopey lately? That didn't give her the right to commit hair homicide on her best friend.

"Yeah," I said, "maybe." Was there a patron saint of hair—St. Pantene, perhaps? Someone to whom I could offer prayers? Burn incense in front of? Sacrifice older brothers to?

"In fact, I bet if you brush it out again really hard, it'll relax a little right away." She tentatively touched my hair but visibly recoiled. Who wouldn't? This wasn't hair any longer. It was a hundred slinkies attached to my head—a head that smelled like scorched fruit.

"Umm, it's getting dark. Maybe my dad can take you home," she said. We both had heard him come in a half hour ago.

Kerrie rarely asked her dad to drive her or her friends anywhere. The fact that she was going to ask him to take me home told me precisely what she thought of my hairstyle—a total disaster. It was like a polygraph scratching out the truth—my hair was unsuitable for public consumption.

While I fought back tears of self-pity, Kerrie rushed downstairs and returned a few seconds later to say it was okay, he'd take me home. When I went downstairs with her, Mr. Daniels stood by the front door with his keys in hand, but his gaze said more than I wanted to know. He looked at my hair more than at me and seemed confused. Finally, he said, "Are you in a play or something, Bianca?"

I refrained from bursting out sobbing and just shook my head, "no." Kerrie accompanied me on the ride and made a noble attempt to keep a conversation going. But all I could think of was how I'd fix my hair, or even *if* I could fix it. And if I couldn't, I wondered if there was some sort of leave of absence I could take from school until the perm grew out.

The first sign that I was right was when I got home and my mother didn't yell at me for being late. I was supposed to fix dinner that night—we take turns since Mom works—so being late wasn't just being late. It was "no dinner when dinner was supposed to be ready" late.

16

But Mom took one look at my hair, her mouth dropped open, maybe her eyes watered, too, and she sucked in her lips. I could smell the meatloaf already baking, which meant she'd put it on herself. Yet, she said not one word about my cooking duties. Instead, she merely told me when dinner would be ready and asked me how my day was.

"I think you can see how it was!" I moaned, touching my hair. A few singed ends came off in my hand.

"Where did you get it done?" she asked. "Maybe you can get a refund."

"Kerrie did it for me. No refund."

"Why don't you go take a shower? It might relax a little if you wash it."

I tramped upstairs to my room, threw my backpack on the bed, and avoided looking at myself in the mirror above my dresser. My sister Connie's door was closed, and music was wafting into the hallway. Tony was nowhere to be seen. At least I'd be able to zip into the bathroom without running smack into sibling cruelty. Call me crazy, but I don't think I'd get the same kind of loving sympathy from them as I got from Mom.

This was borne out at dinner a little while later. I showed up at the table in my robe with a towel, arranged swami-style, around my head.

Connie looked at me with narrowed eyes and asked me if I was sick or something, but Mom cut her off by saying I took a shower after school. Tony sniffed the air and said something smelled funny. He was right. The perm's odor had been intensified by warm water. My head was surrounded by an aura of putrid foulness, like a garbage dump left in the sun. Boy, was I happy!

Or not. I was pretty bummed. But have you noticed how hunger can often mask other emotions—such as bummedness? Since Mom made the meatloaf, it was actually good, so we all dove in. Literally. When we're all hungry, the Balducci table is not a place for the faint-hearted. Tony started jabbing at the meat while Connie piled her plate with potatoes and carrots (she's into vegetables) and I snagged a couple of rolls for mine. Poor Mom had nothing on her plate until we were all done whooshing and zooming the dishes between us so fast our table could have qualified for federal funding for air traffic controllers.

Although we kids prefer to watch television during dinner, Mom has this pesky rule about actually talking to each other. She started the ball rolling by asking us each about our days.

"Fine," Tony mumbled through a mouthful of meat. Tony was an unapologetic carnivore.

"Mmm . . . mmm . . . too," Connie said, which I guess meant "me too have fine day, ugh."

Since Mom was nice to me, I stepped up to the plate and recounted my afternoon in such detail she probably regretted asking the question. By the time I was done reciting my litany of woes about Kerrie and Sarah and Doug (leaving out the perm, of course—I have *some* pride), Tony was rolling his eyes.

"Flypaper for freaks," he announced. "That's what you are, Bianca—flypaper for freaks." He edged the meatloaf his way and cut himself a third slice. The main course was nearly gone now.

"Tony, don't talk about your sister that way," said Mom.

At least part of my story was interesting enough to get Connie's attention. Since she's a private investigator, she wanted to know about the police action at the museum. Unfortunately, I didn't have anything to tell her other than "cops-arrive-at-museum." Oh . . . and one other thing.

"They might be looking for a private investigator," I said smugly, knowing she'd love to land another assignment. "Don't know why."

"Hmm . . . that's interesting," she said, trying not to sound too interested so I wouldn't think I'd done her a favor.

After dinner, I volunteered to clean up, but Mom was still being nice to me, so she helped. There weren't many leftovers to put away, and after I'd loaded the dishwasher and she'd determined I didn't have much homework, she told me I could get on the Internet if I wanted to.

I could have burst out crying.

Not only had she not yelled at me for being late and not fixing dinner, she had helped me clean up *and* told me I could have Internet privileges when we have dial-up service that ties up the phone. This perm was not just bad. To generate this kind of pity, it had to be atrociously awful.

I decided the best thing to do about it, though, was to use an avoidance strategy. So I kept the towel on my head all evening—through my hour of homework and through the two hours I spent online. Yup, I spent 120 minutes in cyberspace, and didn't feel even a wee bit guilty for hogging the phone line all that time. I deserved it for the suffering inflicted on my head that afternoon.

Mostly I chatted with friends through instant messages and e-mails. In between, I did some research for a project due right before Christmas break.

Curiously, Kerrie wasn't online and neither was Doug. Usually, I could count on Doug being online virtually any night of the week, and I really wanted to chat with him. Even more curious was the fact that Sarah *was* online. Despite the fact that Kerrie and she were supposed to share Internet privileges, Kerrie got the lion's share of time and I rarely saw Sarah online. When I popped her an IM, she came back quickly with "can't talk. trying to get into college," which meant she was doing research for college apps.

Although I had some fun talking with other friends, I was bothered enough by not seeing my boyfriend and best friend online that I got off the computer even before anyone asked me to. (Okay, even before they yelled at me to.)

Picking up the phone, expecting to hear the beep-beep-beep signaling the existence of voice mail messages (one would surely be from Doug), I was disappointed again. Just the drone of the dial tone greeted me. Should I call him? Heck no! I had too much pride. Besides, I was afraid I'd break down sobbing if I told him about my hair.

Chapter Three

That night I had what I think is called a "wish fulfillment" dream. I dreamt I was laughing and running through a flowery meadow high in the hills where trees rustled in the late day sun, a waterfall gurgled cheerfully in the distance, cool breezes kissed my cheek, and multicolored iridescent butterflies flitted around my flowing locks. You get the picture—I had normal hair. But when I woke up and touched my head, the dream evaporated faster than a morning fog.

Showering had not straightened it, or relaxed it, or done anything to it except, if this was possible, to make it look even frizzier. I thought maybe sleeping on it would have helped as well—kind of mashing it down so it didn't look so fierce. All sleeping on it did, though, was create a dent on the right side. Very attractive.

I pulled out a bandana and tied it on. Frizzy ends still poked out from underneath, but the blue-print triangle of cloth contained some of the damage.

When I went downstairs for breakfast, Tony gave me a weird look, as if he wasn't sure what was different about me, then went back to snarfing down his cornflakes.

Mom had already left for her office, and Connie was in the shower.

"Weird" must have been in my horoscope because when I went to grab some milk from the refrigerator, I came face to face with yet another strange occurrence.

About a week before Thanksgiving, I'd received in the mail some promotional thing for a girl's magazine. Included in it were poetry magnets. I didn't order the magazine, but I did keep the magnets. Before going to bed the night before, I'd put up this hopeful message on the fridge: "geek girl turns glam/crush is real man." Hey, with so few words, there weren't that many possible arrangements, okay? And besides, it had made me feel better after my thermonuclear hair day.

But when I checked the fridge in the morning, someone had rearranged the little rectangles and used other words to spell out: "chill glam girl/real groove is messy."

"Who changed my poem?" I asked Tony as I drank a glass of Instant Breakfast. I'm not much of a breakfast person. I'm lucky if I can tolerate a bowl of Frosted Flakes in the morning, while Connie consumes healthy stuff like granola and fruit slushes, and Tony sometimes grabs a McMuffin on the way into class.

"Huh? I dunno. Probably Connie." He didn't even look at me but kept his eyes on the morning newspaper.

Connie came in a few seconds later, opened the fridge, and poured herself some orange juice. She sniffed at the open refrigerator.

"Something stinks in here. We need to clean it out."

Oh, man. It was my hair. I was getting used to the smell, but others could detect its killer odors from across a room.

Connie looked at me, tilted her head, drank her juice, then issued her verdict. "Wow. Bad perm, huh?"

I shrugged my shoulders, which in Balducci language means "Yeah. Kerrie did it. What could I do? I'm mortified, so leave me alone."

"You ready?" Tony asked. He was driving me to school. He placed his bowl in the sink.

I slurped the last of my chocolate drink, and reached down for my backpack.

"Just a sec." I turned to Connie. "Why did you change the poem?"

"Huh? What poem?" Connie stared at me like I was a lunatic. Come to think of it, she often stared at me that way.

"On the refrigerator door. My poem."

She turned to face the door, which was covered with newspaper clippings, coupons, and menus for Chinese and Italian carry-outs. The competing messages were too much for her. She said nothing.

"C'mon. Let's get going," Tony said. "You're going to make me late again."

I sometimes wonder what Tony will do when he doesn't have me or Connie to blame things on any more. Ignoring his impatience, I raced back up to my room, pulled down the bandana, and spritzed Heaven cologne on my hair. Maybe that would mask the odor, I thought. One could only hope.

Back downstairs, the front door was open, which meant Tony was already outside revving up the car. I yelled a goodbye to Connie and she returned the affectionate farewell with her own chipper "Don't forget, you're fixing dinner tonight since you messed up last night!" and I was off to school.

Tony gave me a few sideways glances en route, like he was still trying to figure out what was different about me. My guess was he didn't even remember what color hair I had, let alone whether it was curly or straight. Tony's goal in life was to become a millionaire. I got the distinct impression he saw his family members solely as obstacles to that goal.

After he dropped me at school, I rushed into the locker hall to dump my stuff and get ready for first period—Western Civ. Kerrie was nowhere to be seen, which was odd, because we usually hooked up in the locker hall before school, especially on days like this one, when we didn't have many classes together. Sarah was there, though, and that meant Kerrie was someplace nearby since they usually came in together. Sarah had her own car.

"Wow," Sarah said, looking at my hair. "What happened to *you?*"

"An unfortunate incident involving my hair and a permanent wave set."

"What made you do that?" she asked, twirling her combination lock. "Nobody does perms any more."

"Call me a rugged individualist, I guess." I didn't see any point in laying the blame at Kerrie's feet. She'd only been trying to help.

Trying to help or not, Kerrie was probably avoiding me because she felt guilty. Now, I could forgive her for the perm disaster, but I was annoyed that she'd stay out of my way because of the guilts.

"Where's Kerrie?" I asked as I stashed my lunch bag and grabbed some books.

"Don't know. She had her dad drive her in."

Uh-oh. If Kerrie had her father give her a ride, that meant she was miffed at Sarah big-time. This was getting tiresome. I might need to fly in a negotiator and work out a truce.

"Did you get hold of Connie?" I said as casually as I could. "I didn't get a chance to talk to her last night."

"No," Sarah said. "I didn't. But I did give her number to Ms. Dexter."

"I thought you said they already had a private investigator working on something."

"I don't think she signed anything with him. I think she's shopping around."

"Well, thanks. Connie'll be happy to get the work." I leaned against the locker. "But what's it for, anyway?"

"I'm still not sure."

"Why'd the alarm go off yesterday—is it connected to that?"

"I don't know. Everybody's being cagey. Even Hector." She grimaced.

"You said you overheard your boss mentioning him. Are you afraid he's in trouble?"

Sarah shook her head. "No! I'm just afraid if something's wrong, they'll point fingers at him because . . . well, because he's a Latino . . ."

"Yeah, but what's wrong? What's going on there?" This was getting frustrating. I took a deep breath. "Just tell me what you know, what you've seen."

She frowned and looked around again as if afraid someone would overhear.

"They seem to be doing a lot of 'restoration' work lately. On new stuff, modern stuff, that doesn't need restoration, okay?"

How was I supposed to know? I was lucky if I could draw a stick figure without giving it three eyes. Come to think of it, that might qualify as modern art, so maybe I wasn't out of my league after all.

"If it's really new, I can't imagine why they'd need to—

what do you mean by restoration work, anyway?" Frustration gave way to curiosity. I felt the hair on the back of my neck stand up. Or, actually, frizz up.

"They have a room where they touch up old paintings. Artists do it, with some art students helping out. It's neat. I've seen them work."

"So that's why your boss is looking into hiring a private investigator—because the new stuff is deteriorating too fast?" Maybe they didn't need Connie. Maybe they needed an environmental protection agent. It sounded like something was toxic in that museum.

"No. Well, yeah. I mean . . . I think Ms. Dexter is having stuff restored to check it out. To make sure it's real."

I felt like hitting my head with my hand. "Forgery! That's what you think has happened. Someone has forged some new works and they're privately checking it out!"

"That's why I thought she should call Connie. The guy she's been talking to—well, every time she gets off the phone with him, she goes looking for Hector and starts asking him questions."

Sarah's convoluted explanation left me hankering for more information, but just then, just as the sands of time had almost finished drifting through the time-before-class hourglass, Kerrie rolled in—with Doug! With Doug's arm around her shoulder! Hey, this wasn't fair! Her eyes were red and her face streaked, which meant she'd been crying.

"Kerrie, what's the matter?" I asked, rushing to her side. Sarah hung back.

"She had a fight with her dad," Doug said.

I got the picture—they both arrived at school at the same time, Doug saw her crying, and Doug, being a good guy, tried to comfort her. Good old Doug. So why did this make me uneasy?

Kerrie thanked Doug and went to her locker, but the look Doug threw her way was enough to send up alarm bells. Doug was a softie. And I was beginning to get impatient with Kerrie.

"What happened this time?" I asked, maybe a tad too snappily.

Doug looked at my hair, probably for the first time, and I could have sworn he curled his lip. "Kerrie told me about your hair, Bianca. It *will* grow out."

I felt my face grow warm from an angry blush. Kerrie told Doug about my hair? And not only that, she must have told him about it in such a way that he was predisposed to dislike it! She stole my comfort! Doug was supposed to console *me*, not her! This was a gyp! I wanted a refund. I was the one who had first dibs on Doug's comfort!

"It's not that bad," I said defensively.

"I think it's kind of cute," Sarah said, lightly fingering the frizzy ends sticking out from under my bandana. Some fell off in her hand, and she wiped them on her skirt.

Doug said nothing. Kerrie sniffled.

"What happened with your dad?" I asked.

"Oh, nothing," she said, turning her lock.

The buzzer screeched, signaling we were supposed to be in our homerooms. To heck with that—they always gave us a few minutes grace time, and I was not leaving until I got some information, or at least a kind word from Doug.

"It had to be something. You were crying." I moved in closer to Kerrie.

27

"It's nothing, really!" Kerrie grabbed her books and slammed the locker door shut. "I have to go. I'm going to be late. That's the last thing I need today!"

After she left, I looked at Doug and raised my eyebrows, which in Balducci language meant, "What the hey is going on here?"

Sarah seemed to be thinking the same thing, because she hovered nearby, awaiting Doug's explanation. He disappointed us both.

"I don't know. You better get it from her," he said, then ran off to class with a quick "later" in my direction and an affectionate punch to my arm.

Sarah and I shrugged, and she ran off to class, too.

I felt like sitting down and crying. I'd wanted more information from Sarah about the ruckus at the museum, but got sidetracked by Kerrie's mysterious crying jag, and Doug's touching but misdirected sympathy.

And, oh yes, it *was* misdirected. I was supposed to be soaking up the sympathy because of my hair. When I hadn't been able to reach Doug last night, I had worked myself into a buzz thinking about how darned sympathetic he'd be when I rested my head on his shoulder and sobbed out the story of the misguided perm. But Kerrie had sucked his sympathy dry! There was none left for me.

Feeling sad, annoyed, and curious, I stomped off to class.

Chapter Four

My day went from bad to worse. First, in Western Civ, I found out I had written a deadline in my notebook wrong, which meant that while all the other students handed in their papers on the causes of World War II, I was left sitting as unprepared as the French had been at the Maginot line because I'd thought the paper was due the week before Christmas. Then, when I told the teacher about my mistake after class, he just shrugged and said, "if you get it in by the end of the week, I'll take just one grade level off." *One grade level?* Great. That meant I'd have to write an A-plus paper just to get a B-plus. That's a real motivation spiker, let me tell ya.

Later, in chorus, Mr. Baker spent virtually the entire session lecturing us in a "how could you?" tone of voice about the number of "please excuse my son/daughter . . ." notes he was receiving from kids who wanted out of the Christmas concert. Hey, it was scheduled on the last day of classes and a bunch of kids were taking off for their grandparents. Families are spread all over the country now, but I guess in ol' Baker's day, they'd stayed close to the central hearth.

Later in that class, I saw Sarah and managed to pass her a note asking if she'd thought any more about Kerrie's party. Mr. Baker, meanwhile, took us through a rendition of "Feeling Groovy" because he wanted to do some "popular music" in the spring. Yup. Popular music. Maybe when he was a kid. Hmm . . . Mr. Baker as a kid. I saw him in knee pants and bow tie . . . Anyway, Baker caught Sarah trying to write me back and made her put away her notebook.

And finally, I happened to see Kerrie later that morning heading into study hall—with Doug! Doug talking to her real confidential-like, leaning down toward her. And she looked all weepy-eyed again, which meant she was still vacuuming up all his sympathy supply, and again leaving none for me!

So my morning was a linear progression from goofy teacher, to information void, to potential heartbreak.

Maybe lunch would be better, right?

Wrong. Whatever happened with Kerrie and her dad had ratcheted up her animosity toward Sarah. For the first time since enrolling with me at St. John's, Kerrie spent a lunch hour at another table. When I saw her heading for a group of girls in her homeroom, I cheerily waved her over to our usual table at the back of the bright-white cafeteria near the doors to the auditorium lobby.

"Sorry, Bianca," she said kind of coldly, "I have a group project due before Christmas and I thought I'd get a head start on it."

Since when does any student use lunch period to get a head start on a class project?

Normally, I would have tried to nudge Kerrie back into the straight and narrow path of our friendship. But today, after seeing how she'd used my boyfriend as a sympathy sop, I decided I couldn't care less who she ate lunch with as long as it wasn't Doug.

Then Sarah plopped down at my table with a tray loaded up for a nuclear winter—pizza, salad, corn chips, a giant chocolate chip cookie, and a container of milk. I opened my bag and pulled out my PB&J on nearly stale whole wheat. We only eat whole wheat bread at my house because of Connie's fascination with health food. If I want white bread, I have to bring it in special, like contraband shipped across enemy lines.

"Mrs. Taney made a comment about your bandana," Sarah said as she opened her milk carton. "She's not sure it's legal."

"Gee, thanks, Sarah. Maybe you want to go eat with Kerrie, too, huh?" I was in no mood for teasing, or even a "helpful" heads-up from a friend warning me of a potential dress code violation and detention.

"Whoa. Calm down. I'm just trying to help. You might want to stay away from Taney, that's all." Sarah looked over at Kerrie and her eyes narrowed.

"Okay. I give up," I said after washing my sandwich down with a half liter of iced tea. "What's happening with Kerrie, and let's talk some more about the museum thing, okay?" That's what I needed—other people's problems to keep my mind off my own.

"I still don't know what's up with Kerrie. Doug might know, though. She seemed to be talking to him a lot today." Although Sarah said it noncommittally, I couldn't help wondering if she was trying to plant seeds of doubt in my mind about Kerrie. After all, if she and Kerrie were in Tension Universe, she might want to have me in her Command Central, aligned against Kerrie. Hmm . . . I really did need that negotiator, or special envoy, or *someone*, for crying out loud.

On to Topic Number Two, which I was increasingly interested in because my motto was fast becoming "when in doubt, snoop."

"What did the cops find when they came to the museum yesterday?" I asked.

Sarah wiped her mouth and broke off a piece of cookie. She obviously subscribed to the life advice about eating dessert first. I liked that advice, too. I wished I'd had some dessert with which to implement it, but I only had an apple, and an apple just isn't the same thing as a cookie—I don't care what nutritionists tell you.

"Some alarm tripped. Nothing special. Electrical snafu or something."

"Who told you that?"

"Hector." As soon as she said it, her face reddened. Hector—the "Latino" she was afraid her boss was fingering for . . . whatever.

"Is Hector a good worker?"

"Yeah! Why do you ask?"

"Just wondering if that's why you overheard your boss talking about him—you know, complaining."

"I don't know why she was talking about him. That's part of the problem!" Clearly, talking about this upset Sarah. She suspected something, but was afraid to voice it. I'd have to back up and get her to calm down if I wanted to get more out of her.

Ever since I got involved in Sarah's own mystery earlier in the fall, I found I had a hankering for mysteries in general. I thought I might have some talent in that regard—figuring things out. And I wanted my sister Connie to hire me to help out in her fledgling private eye business next summer. It would be a lot better than working at Burger Boy, which was Tony's place of part-time employment. And a lot better than baby-sitting, which was what my mother was trying to line up for me.

Me as a babysitter? That had disaster written all over it. The only thing I knew about miniature people was that they leaked—their noses ran, their mouths drooled, and other parts were always wet and needing changing. Not the right kind of job for "glam girl."

No, I saw myself in trench coat and Fedora finding Maltese Falcons and kidnapped heiresses. Which brought me back to the museum, Sarah, and Hector.

"Does your boss know that you and Hector are friends?" I asked.

"No. Don't think so. It's all business in the office. I stay pretty busy. And Hector has his rounds and all."

"So when do you get to talk to him?"

"On his breaks. He takes his breaks outside in this small parking lot in the back. Next to the dumpster."

Wow. How romantic. A rendezvous near the dumpster.

"Does your boss see you?"

"No. Why?"

"Well, if she doesn't know you're friends with Hector, you might be able to get some info out of her. Ask her some pointed questions."

Sarah brightened. "Like what?"

"Well, you could get her talking about the alarm. Ask her if she suspects foul play—if someone tripped it on purpose."

"Yeah." Sarah liked that idea, and frankly, so did I. While I had every intention of pumping my sister for info if she got the museum job, I also could use my own powers of investigation—by using Sarah as my agent, my plant, my mole—my *whatever!*

"And then you could casually ask her if they ever had

that problem before—someone tripping the alarm. And then kind of casually say something like 'who would even know how to do that—the guards?' and see what she says, see if she says anything about Hector." I was getting excited about this. I knew exactly how I would handle the investigation. I could even envision myself "casually" asking all those questions.

"Thanks, Bianca. I'll try that the next time I'm there."

Okay, that mystery was percolating, so onto the next one—like what was up with Kerrie. After gulping down my sandwich, which was no mean feat considering it was dry as kindling, I sashayed over to Kerrie's new lunch table. I didn't care what she thought. I was going to get to the bottom of this. Hmm . . . this hair thing had an "up" side. It was emboldening me, giving me a devil-may-care attitude about life. I mean, after you suffer through hair humiliation, the only way to go is up, right?

"Kerrie, do you have a sec?" I asked, standing next to her table. She looked surprised.

"Uh. Yeah. What do you want?"

"I need to talk to you. Privately."

Reddening, she stood and followed me out of the caf to the dim lobby in front of the auditorium. Maybe she was motivated by fear that I would berate her about my hair in front of her new friends, warning them to stay away from the newest Hair Terminator. "See what she's done to me? Go back! Go back!" I could have yelled, ripping the bandana from my head with a flourish. Hmm . . . not a bad scenario. I'd have to remember it in case Kerrie continued to act goofy.

"What?" she asked, folding her arms across her chest.

"What's up with you?" I asked. "You come into school all weepy, then sit with others at lunch. Did I do something?" Of course I didn't do anything. She's the

one who did something. But I needed to ask this question to make her wrong-headed attitude completely
clear to her.

"No, you didn't! It's just that . . ." Her eyes started to
water and I wanted to scream. Here we go again.
"Sarah. You're sitting with Sarah. And she did something really nasty to me last night."

I mentally rolled my eyes. Okay, maybe I really rolled
my eyes. But I made sure Kerrie wasn't looking when I
did it. "What did she do?" I asked, trying to sound understanding but not too sympathetic.

"She roped my dad into taking her to Boston for the
weekend."

With that one sentence, I had the full picture. Here it is:
Mr. Daniels suggests to Sarah that she look at a few
Boston-area colleges. He sets up the appointments. Kerrie asks him to take her somewhere. He reveals his other
plans. She blames Sarah since she can't bring herself to
blame Dad. And when she expresses her disappointment,
Dad chides her. Big argument. Tears. Doug sympathy.

"Well, Ker, she *is* applying to colleges kind of late," I
said as gently as I could. "But she'll be finished with it
soon enough. And look at it this way—your dad is learn-
ing a lot about how to help you with it when your time
comes."

This did not help. In fact, if anything, it seemed to
make Kerrie madder.

"That's what my father said!" she fumed. "But that's
not the point. We always go Christmas shopping together the weekend after Thanksgiving weekend. And
now he won't even be in town!"

All right, I'm a softie. Despite the fact that Kerrie was
being obtuse (I just learned that word in English class, by
the way—it can mean "insensitive" and "stupid"), she

35

and I went back a long ways. Well, since freshman year, anyway. Looking at her now, I thought of how hard it must be to adjust to siblinghood after living in Only Child Land for so long. I thought of what a good relationship she had with her dad. Who was I to scoff at that? My dad died when I was too young to know him. If he was around, I'd probably be guarding my moments with him like a sentry, too, right? Maybe we didn't need a special negotiator flown in. Maybe I just needed to be a better friend.

"Why don't you go shopping with *me?*" I asked tentatively. Then I reached over and squeezed her arm. She smiled ruefully (another new word, it means "mournfully" or "regretfully").

"Thanks, Bianca. That's sweet of you. Maybe."

"Doug and I were supposed to go to the mall this weekend," I continued. "You could come along."

"Yeah, he mentioned that."

Screeching halt to the Sympathy Train. Doug mentioned our mall date? As in "why don't you come along on it"? No, no, no! This was all wrong. Doug, being the boyfriend, could not open our dates up to other girls without permission from me. He could only open them up to other boys. I, the girlfriend, was the designated inviter of other girls. Hadn't he read the dating rules book? Did he need some remedial work here?

"Uh. That's good," I said, pasting a smile on my face. "I'll call you about a time."

"He said noonish."

Splat. That was the sound of my heart hitting the floor. Doug even told her the time? He hadn't even told *me* that!

"Yeah. Noonish," I sputtered. Just then, the buzzer

deafened us. It was time to clear out and head to the next class.

"Thanks, Bianca. You made me feel better," Kerrie said as we headed back into the cafeteria to get our things. "And don't worry about your hair. Doug said that's not why he likes you, anyway."

If that was supposed to be comforting, it failed miserably. By the time I arrived at my next class, Honors Geometry, I was convinced Kerrie and Doug had a secret thing going, and she'd ruined my hair on purpose.

Chapter Five

For a guy to comment on a girl's hair, it had to be really, really good or really, really bad. Doug really, really didn't like my hair. That had to be the case if he'd mentioned it to Kerrie. That lame "that's not why he likes you, anyway" line that Kerrie had thrown at me told the whole story. His misguided attempts at sympathy later in the day clinched my case. Outside after school, before heading to his bus, he talked to me, but he kept looking at my hair while he talked and his eyes kept scrunching up kind of funny, like he expected it to reach out and grab him or something.

And when he left, he didn't do his usual peck-on-the-cheek-when-no-one's-looking thing or even his funny punch-me-in-the-arm thing. He just said, "I'll be in touch."

"Be in touch"? Like he was going on the Grand Tour or something and would send me a postcard? Something was amiss here.

So, all the way home by myself on the bus (since Sarah had to go to the museum again and Kerrie was getting a ride with some seniors), I moped my way through the logic of my relationship with Doug. And it led nowhere good.

Not liking the hair was making him not like me, or at least not want to be seen in a public display of affection toward me. So who wants a boyfriend whose affection rests solely on how good you looked? I mean, what if I was disfigured in an accident? Would he not stand by me?

I was going from Doug not wanting me to me not wanting Doug. Who wants a shallow-minded boyfriend, anyway?

I do, that's who. (Or should that be "whom?")

Sniffling, I got off my bus and walked the block to my house, throwing my backpack on the hallway floor and heading for the kitchen.

On the table was a note from my mother. "Preheat oven to 350. Wash chicken. Put in roaster pan at 4:30. Cook rice and vegetable. Love, Mom."

When I went to get myself a consolation glass of chocolate milk, I noticed the poetry magnets had been changed yet again.

"Clueless friend/Totally flirt/Feel hot/dream psyched."

"Connie!" I yelled. To my surprise, she answered.

"What?!" she called from upstairs. After waiting a second to see if she'd come down, I gave in and trudged upstairs to her room. Standing in her doorway, I watched as she buckled a leather belt around a short khaki skirt, and fastened gold hoop earrings to her ears. Normally, she was a jeans and tee kind of dresser—just one more reason why I wanted to follow in her footsteps to become a private eye. No pantyhose required.

"Why did you change my poem?" I asked as she tugged on stacked-heel, mahogany-colored leather boots.

"What is it with you and the poems? Are you going nuts?" She grabbed a jacket that matched her skirt and shrugged her shoulders into it.

"How come you're home? And why so dressed up?"

She walked to her mirror above her dresser and spritzed on some Christian Dior cologne. Then she ran a brush through her short, dark—and naturally wavy—hair.

"Appointment with a client. I came home to change." Connie was trying hard to build up a big enough business so she could afford her own place. Having to live with us put a real crimp in her life, especially her love life. She was seeing a guy named Kurt, who looked like a good-hearted muscleman and helped her out of tight spots. He'd helped me out of a couple, too, in the fall.

She grabbed a big leather bag that matched her boots, and threw some folders and papers into it. She looked so focused and happy that I wanted to grab a piece of her bag.

"Did someone from the museum call you—about an alarm being set off?" I blurted out.

"You know I can't say . . ."

"Sarah told me."

"All right. Yeah. A Fawn Dexter called."

"So you're on the case?"

Connie smiled, a kind smile—the smile that says she's happy enough about something to be distracted from her usual sibling persecution regimen.

"Yeah, so thanks, if you had anything to do with it."

"Can I help you with it?"

"Look, there is no 'it.' Or hardly any 'it" at all. Which is why I have to go. Need to drum up new business. We can talk later."

As she brushed past me, she added, "And by the way, the alarm was tripped accidentally. That's all."

"I already knew that!" I said, following her.

"Well, I guess you knew that it helped turn up something else." She ran downstairs and grabbed her car keys from the half-table by the door. I ran after her.

"Yeah, as a matter of fact, I did. I knew all about it."

She paused while she checked her bag to make sure she had everything, and it was clear she wasn't listening to me, or didn't believe me. "Some art students accidentally tripped the alarm," she said, not looking at me. "But when the cops came out, they found some weird stuff."

"I know. Like modern art pieces that might be a little too modern, if you know what I mean."

She was heading to the door and I suddenly became afraid that she wouldn't tell me—that this was just a continuation of "National Be Cruel to Bianca Day." But she stopped and looked up, and . . . and noticed my hair. It did the trick. Her eyes filled with sympathy. And so she had to spill the beans. Maybe having bad hair wasn't so bad after all.

"One of the art students claimed her stuff was missing. But it was no big deal. It just wasn't where she left it." Connie looked at her watch. "I gotta run. Don't forget to put on dinner."

After she left in a cloud of too-much-cologne, I kicked my backpack. She'd given me hardly any new information. So what if some art student forgot her paints or something? I was hoping for a juicy scoop I could share with Sarah.

Dragging my backpack into the kitchen, I sat at the table and pulled out my books. But I nixed the idea of working. I mean, come on! I had the house to myself for a couple hours before Tony and Mom came home, and who knew when Connie would be back? The computer and the phone were screaming out for me to use them. I opted for the computer, and before you could say "beam me up," I was logged on and surfing.

Within a few seconds, Sarah IMed me.

"aren't you at work?" I asked her.

"yeah, but i'm researching something for a press release. wassup?"

"nothin." But then I remembered Connie's info, so I shared it with Sarah.

"hmmm . . ." she IMed back. Then, "big party here sunday. wanna come?"

"what party?"

"exhibit opening. i could get you in. and doug too."

Doug and me at the art museum? I envisioned soft music, classy food, sophisticated conversation. Culture could be romantic. I liked it.

"sure, what time?"

After we made arrangements, my mood lifted exponentially. The mall date might be muddied by Kerrie's presence, but the museum date—that would be a real treat. Just me and Doug and all that culture. Oh yeah, and about a hundred patrons of the museum. But they'd be strangers, so it would be like Doug and I were alone, right?

"thought you'd be in boston on sunday, though," I typed back, remembering the college trip.

"yeah, well . . ." she responded. Uh-oh. Sounded like Kerrie problems again. I didn't feel up to that, so we then IMed each other about a bunch of inconsequential stuff, after which she suddenly threw a hardball at me.

"if you had a friend who you thought had done something wrong, what would you do?"

"is this a religion assignment?" I IMed back quickly.

"no"

"do you know if the friend definitely did something wrong, or are you just wondering?"

"wondering. sort of."

What the hey did that mean?

"then maybe you should talk to them."

"i don't want to accuse them or anything."

Hmm . . . was she talking about her boss and those Flirt Voice conversations? I had learned my lesson in the fall about not waiting to confront friends in trouble. But what about confronting an adult you suspect might be fooling around? Naw, I just didn't see it.

"if you're not sure they did something wrong, maybe you should just let it be."

"even if you saw clues?"

Clues to what? I wanted to scream.

"it depends. maybe we can talk about this."

I chatted with Sarah and a couple other friends for about an hour or so, blithely ignoring my mother's "half hour" rule for the phone. I was still enjoying my post-perm grace period. She'd forgive me. I was sure of it.

Or not. When the last friend typed "g2g" ("got to go" for you cyber-challenged folks), I shrieked because of the time—4:50! And I hadn't put the chicken in the oven! Maybe Mom would be late, I thought, as I rushed to turn the oven on (to 400—maybe cooking it higher would cook it faster). I rinsed the chicken, did my Emeril imitation (bam! bam!) with the salt and pepper, popped the fowl in the roasting pan, and slammed the door shut. Then I got out a saucepan and pulled out some Rice-a-Roni, which is a staple of our diet. For years, I thought rice's natural color was orange.

After getting that started, I tossed some frozen corn

into another pan, then rushed to set the table, being careful to fold the napkins perfectly so Mom would think I really labored over them.

Good thing, too, because she didn't arrive late. She arrived early, just two minutes after I managed to get everything in progress. She sniffed the air after she called out her greeting, and at first I thought it was my darn perm, but no, she was smelling for dinner.

"Bianca, did you put that chicken in?" she asked, coming into the kitchen. She was dressed in a navy blue pant suit, and I thought she looked pretty good. She was still fairly slender, and had soft brown hair and pale blue eyes.

"Sure thing, Mom," I said, smiling. But then she went over, opened the door, and saw those pale slimy pieces staring at her. The gig was up. Well, almost.

"At 4:30?" she pressed.

"Well, I kind of didn't put the oven on at 4:30." Okay, so it was a white lie. But I wasn't actually saying anything blatantly untrue. Sure, I didn't put the chicken in until a few minutes ago. But I knew that if she thought I just forgot to turn the oven on and the chicken had been in the oven at the right time, she'd give me points for effort.

She grimaced but said, "Okay." Taking off her jacket and draping it over a kitchen chair, she gave me a long stare. "If you want, I can get an appointment for you at Hair Force One on Saturday," she said. "They could cut off the worst of it."

I reached up and touched it again. "I was thinking of trying to wash it tonight one more time. Maybe try a straightener."

Mom shook her head. "I don't think you should put anything else on it yourself. You need a professional."

She grabbed the phone book and started flipping through the pages.

"I'm supposed to go to the mall with Doug on Saturday. Around noon," I said.

She punched in a number and in a few minutes had some receptionist on the line. Within a minute or two after that, she was telling her my tale of woe. A few seconds later, she got off.

"After school, Friday," she said.

"I was thinking of going shopping then."

"I thought you said you were going to the mall on Saturday."

"Yeah, but I have to get Doug a Christmas gift, and I can't do that with him in tow."

"You can do that another time," my mother said. "We're going to Aunt Rosa's for dinner Friday night."

Ouch. She thought my hair looked so bad she didn't want to be seen in public with me. Even at Aunt Rosa's. I left the room to go take a look.

Leaving the room turned out to be a big mistake. You see, while I tended to my hair, which mostly consisted of staring at it in my bedroom mirror and imagining it looking lots different, Mom assumed I was still tending to dinner. But since she was home, I assumed she would be tending to it. Which meant we were all summoned to the dinner table by the sound of the smoke alarm going off, and our baked chicken turned into barbequed chicken—the charred kind.

Not that Tony minded. That boy would eat anything. In fact, he even complimented me on it. He probably thought I'd done it on the outdoor hibachi.

Connie didn't get in until after dinner, when I was wiping off the last of the pots. She wrinkled up her nose and asked "What's that smell?" before looking at my hair and nodding as if she understood now where the house's burnt odors originated. But before I had a chance to set her straight (for once, my hair was not the source of something stinky), she breezed past me, grabbed a yogurt from the fridge, and started complaining, which is her version of small talk.

I sat down at the computer, which is in our kitchen, and pretended to work so I could listen to her. I like a good rant as much as the next girl.

"Damn jerk. He kept asking me who my partner was!" Connie hooked a chair with her boot toe and pulled it out. Connie operated her business under the name Balducci and Associates, except there were no "associates." I would like to be an "associate." "He wanted to know if there was a man he could talk to!"

"Why? Did he have some, you know, sensitive stuff?"

Connie glared at me like I'd just announced my intention to join the cast of Riverdance.

"He can tell me anything he can tell a guy. It's just a freaking divorce case, for cryin' out loud. Nothing I haven't seen or heard before!"

Connie handled a lot of divorce and worker fraud cases. Lots of people think private eye work is all glamorous snooping and murder-solving, when in reality it's mostly spying on cheating spouses and employees trying to hoodwink their employers.

I let her rant for awhile longer and then, when I'd soaked up enough, went to my room to study and to call Doug. I gave him the lowdown on Sunday's date and, although he didn't sound enthusiastic, we had a nice soulful talk. He ended up giving me all the comfort juice I needed to get me through the night.

Chapter Six

The rest of my week was pretty uneventful, and pretty much consumed with how to mask my hair disaster from the outside world. The bandana thing had to go the next day. Sarah was right. It violated the dress code in some perverse gender-equality way. You see, boys aren't allowed to wear caps or hats in our school, so in order to make things "equal," the powers that be have declared that girls can't wear any head coverings, either.

Now, maybe I'm a little nutso here, but I think the reason the boys can't wear the caps is because it's a symbol of disrespect. You know, that whole backwards baseball cap kind of thing (and yes, I'm ashamed to say that Doug has worn backward baseball caps on occasion, too) is a sort of "in your face" iconoclasm. (Okay, okay, so it's vocab week in English. "Iconoclasm" is attacking settled beliefs or institutions.)

Wearing a bandana, on the other hand, is merely adornment. It has nothing whatsoever to do with attacking institutions, or rebellion of any kind. It's a fashion statement—the height of conformity! I wanted to look nice, just like the other girls!

But this kind of deep thought has not penetrated to

the Founding Mothers of our Dress Code Constitution, and, as Sarah had predicted, Mrs. Taney asked me to remove the bandana on Wednesday afternoon.

When I took it off, Barbara Jaworski fainted. Fell like a tree right in the back of English class, and barely missed hitting her head on the folding table with our English projects. Boy, was I ever embarrassed! I started saying "I'm sorry," while Taney rushed to get the nurse.

While I thought there was a cause-and-effect thing going on here, it turns out Barb had a fever and was coming down with the flu. She was sent home early.

On Thursday and Friday, I didn't want to risk any more hair casualties, so I managed to work the wiry strands into two pigtails, which would have been a cute retro style if it weren't for the fact that I don't look good in pigtails.

This whole hair ruckus, though, kept me from focusing too much on the Sarah/Kerrie ruckus, which seemed to quiet down into an uneasy truce. My guess was that Sarah had given in and given up on the Boston trip. Whatever had happened, it did the trick, at least enough for Kerrie and Sarah and I to eat lunch together with some polite, if frosty, conversation about our school work. We scrupulously avoided two subjects—the weekend, and college applications.

I thought a lot about the museum weirdness and even tried to get more out of Connie after school on Thursday, but all she would tell me was that there were some "improprieties" and maybe it was a little deeper than just some misplaced artists' supplies.

"Art theft," I'd announced standing in her doorway, and I could tell from her quick smile that I'd hit the bull's-eye.

"That only happens in books," she said.

"Why else would they be checking out the modern stuff? You don't need to restore something that was just painted, for cryin' out loud."

She said nothing.

"And they've contracted with you because they don't want the police in on it—it would get in the papers. The alarm going off and the cops coming freaked them out." Woohoo! I was figuring it out. Her body language was giving it all away—she was squirming, picking non-existent lint off her skirt.

"The stolen art supplies," I said, suddenly inspired, "was just a cover—something they said to keep the cops from digging deeper."

"Your hair's looking a little better today," she said, emphasizing the "little."

Ah-ha. In Balducci language, her response had meant "You are correct, oh wise younger sibling, but it will cost me too much in pride and honor to admit it, so I must insult you in this sly, subtle way. Please forgive me."

So I had all this to think about as I headed into the weekend.

Ah, the weekend. I was in one of those friend dilemmas. Sunday was the museum shindig Sarah had invited Doug and me to. I was really looking forward to it because not only would I get to be with Doug at some posh get-together, I'd also have a chance to play PI at the "scene of the crime."

The fly in this ointment? Call me crazy, but I don't think Sarah had invited Kerrie. Probably because she knew Kerrie and Doug and I were doing the mall crawl on Saturday together, so we'd have had an opportunity to girlfriend-bond, and Sarah would want Sunday for her own chance at that emotional pie. Plus, Sarah had given up the trip to Boston, so she might not have been feeling very "inviting" to Kerrie. Didn't I tell you I felt like a kid in a bad custody case? Pulled back and forth?

My dilemma—should I mention the museum thing to Kerrie? Or, should I suggest Sarah invite Kerrie, too? And if, as I suspected, Sarah was deliberately leaving Kerrie out of the invite, should I decline to attend as well?

In religion class, we deal often with "love thy neighbor" stuff, but we don't get into real-life details like this. And, as they say, the devil's in the details.

I'd have to think about it. But for now, I put it off. Friday evening was rolling around and I was headed to a hair doctor, then out to dinner, then back home and some blissful time e-mailing Doug, who would be home from his part-time job. Then Saturday, I'd see him in the flesh. Ah, life was good. Moral dilemmas could wait.

On Friday afternoon, right after school, my mother picked me up. The fact that she did this emphasized just how bad this hair thing was. She took off work early to drive to school, chauffeur me to Hair Force One, and back home after I was done. If I thought about this too much, I could get really depressed.

To add to the sense of crisis, as soon as I walked through the door of Hair Force One, the beautician took hold of me as if I were an accident victim entering an emergency room for treatment. "Oh, dear, come right this way. Yes, we were told you'd be coming . . ." Really made me re-evaluate the impression I had made all week and the control I thought I'd mustered over The Hair Situation.

After they tucked me in the chair and placed the plastic apron over me, my mother stood nearby, explaining the perm event, which only added to the atmosphere of medical crisis. During this recitation of the disaster, the beautician nodded sagely while I looked from her to my mother, half expecting someone to connect me to an IV drip and heart monitor. I was beyond caring. I didn't want to wear pigtails any longer. I couldn't wear the bandana. Anything would be better. *Anything*.

For an hour and a half, they shampooed and conditioned and clipped and shaped, and I felt comfortable, my ego-wounds soothed. There's something ultra-relaxing about sitting in a beauty shop chair, having someone fiddle with your hair. The very name—beauty shop—makes you feel pampered and special. As if anyone who walks in looking foul will automatically walk out a beauty. I, for one, was ready to believe.

By the time the beautician—Nell was her name—handed me a mirror to take in the 360 degree view of my new hair, I was ready for small improvements—the frizz tamed, the Brillo controlled, the Annie ratcheted back a notch or two to, oh, "understudy" level maybe. My expectations were modest.

Instead, when I finally let myself look at my new hair with wide open eyes, what I found was, well, what I was aiming for in the first place—casual attractiveness.

I couldn't believe it. My heart started pounding. I thought I heard angels singing. I knelt and kissed the ground Nell walked on.

Well, not really. But I sure was grateful.

My hair was cut short—much shorter than I ever would have opted for on my own—and it was tinted a little with reddish highlights. The frizz was cut off, leaving only waves, nice natural-looking waves that framed my face and trickled down my neck. I was dumbstruck. I was moved.

"Do you like it?" Nell asked.

"Uh. Yes. Yes. A lot," I managed to say. I was already envisioning which earrings would look good with this new style. Maybe big hoops. Or even fake diamond studs—the ones my mom bought from the Avon sales-woman last year. This was perfect. This was hair nirvana. Hair paradise. A little makeup and the right clothes and I would look . . . human!

"Bianca, I've been wanting you to get your hair done like this forever," my mother said, standing next to the chair. "It sets off your face so well."

While she paid for this extravagance, I continued to walk on clouds. Doug would be so impressed. Doug would love it. Everyone would love it.

My mother even listened intently to Nell explaining the benefits of some million-buck shampoo and conditioner, and then—I am not making this up—Mom bought some for me! So this is how gorgeous women lived—buying million-dollar shampoos and hair treatments, having people stare at them in a good way, not the "what's that on your head?" way.

In fact, as soon as we left the shop, I caught a guy staring at me—the "hmmm . . . nice" kind of stare. I sopped it up like a sponge. I was where I wanted to be—in Lovely Land.

I was beginning to wonder if I was dreaming, but when we ended up at my Aunt Rosa's restaurant, yet more manifestations of my altered state occurred. The waiter, who usually made bug eyes at Connie, started hitting on me! He hovered near my place while taking our orders (only a formality at Aunt Rosa's since she told us what was good and we ordered it or suffered family excommunication). He placed the bread basket in front of *me*. Ignoring everyone else, he asked *me* if I would like more iced tea. Even Tony picked up on it and mut-tered something about how I should ask him out. I kicked Tony, of course, while thinking "darn straight he likes me. I'm a babe."

Life was good. And by the time I got home that night and did my IM routine with Doug, I was feeling like nothing, but nothing, could drag me down.

Chapter Seven

Then came Saturday, which started out well enough. Pancakes, made by Mom, Connie in a good mood, Tony silent (hey, what more could I ask for?), and I was still feeling pretty—well—pretty.

I didn't even fret over what to wear. The night before, I'd laid it all out on the one clean spot on my dresser—a khaki skirt (almost like Connie's, but hotter), black long-sleeved tee, gold hoop earrings, and clogs.

Things didn't really start going wrong until right before I left for the mall. I was standing at the door waiting for Doug to pick me up when Connie breezed by.

"Guess you heard," she said, sipping on some herbal tea that smelled almost as bad as my hair the morning before.

"Heard what?"

"That museum thing—now they're fingering some guard."

"What?" A guard—Hector? And fingering him for what? But before she had a chance to answer, I saw Doug pull up and I had to go before he tried to parallel park in the one open spot on the block. I'd seen Doug try to parallel park before. It's not something women and children should watch.

So when I went to the car, I was already feeling out of sorts. Then—more bad vibes! Really bad! Kerrie was sitting in the front seat!

Instead of picking me up first and then going together to retrieve my girlfriend, Doug had violated the first rule of Girlfriend/Boyfriend Regulations—that is, the girlfriend comes first! Always.

When she saw me, Kerrie, a big grin on her face, said, "Here, let me get in the back." But just then a car behind Doug started honking because he was double-parked and I muttered a quick "that's okay" and slid into the backseat. Or I should say, I sulked in the backseat, because that's what I felt like doing. Sulking.

To make matters worse, Kerrie had on an outfit almost identical to mine. Except instead of a miniskirt, she had on tight khaki jeans. But her black long-sleeved tee hugged her body in ways mine never would, so whatever beauty points I got for my hair were canceled out by Kerrie's other points.

Life wasn't fair.

Yes, Doug eventually noticed my hair, but mentioned it only in a perfunctory way, and only after Kerrie said something about it. And I'm not sure he would have said anything at all if she hadn't done a little gushing. Then, he chimed in with a soft "yeah, looks great" and a nod.

So this tainted my entire visit to the mall. It beat in the background of my afternoon like an annoying itch I couldn't scratch. I wanted to get Doug alone so I could be the center of his universe for a few hours. And I wanted to get Kerrie alone so I could tell her I wanted to be alone with Doug. And neither possibility seemed possible.

We took the usual route—from CD store to bookstore to clothes store. But even then Kerrie stole the limelight. I thought I'd get Doug's take on a few dresses for the Mistletoe Dance. Sure, my mom was sewing something special for me, but I knew if I saw something really hot, I could get it and she'd probably say okay. When I saw a black velvet number in The Limited, Kerrie oohed and ahhed over it so much that Doug said maybe she should try it on, too. Need I tell you who filled it out better?

By the time our afternoon was over, I was ready to curl up and cry. At least I had the consolation of knowing that Doug would probably suggest he and I do something alone together that evening. In fact, I viewed the whole Saturday afternoon date as a warm-up to the real thing that evening. I'd even looked at the movie schedule and picked out a few flicks I thought we could catch together.

You can imagine my surprise, then, when he dropped me home first, and not Kerrie! When he first pulled onto my street, I just figured it was another manifestation of Doug's Driving Affliction—he drives slow, is easily distracted, and has an inner compass perpetually askew. He then announced he had to get the car back to his parents because they were going out and their other car was in the shop, so he figured he'd loop around and drop Kerrie off after me.

Because of his lack of parking skills, he once again had to double park, which meant no "walk to the door," no intimate words of regret about not being able to go out together that night (and why didn't he tell me this earlier?—I could have gotten Tony to take us somewhere!), no nothing. At least I was sitting in the front seat by this time. But with Kerrie in the back like some chaperoning grandma, do you think Doug was going to lean over and give me a sweet smooch on the kisser?

"I'll call ya," he said a little wistfully. Yup. *Wistful*'s all I got out of this expedition. And *wistful* does not feed a girl's soul, let me tell ya.

To make matters worse, Connie wasn't home when I came in, so I couldn't pepper her with questions about the museum situation. And I didn't want to call or IM Sarah about it because Connie's little hint about Hector would just upset Sarah. Sarah probably suspected Hector, too, but was too besotted by him to admit it. Sheesh. Life sucked.

The house was as empty as my heart. Mom had left a note saying she was out shopping and there were leftovers in the fridge.

The fridge. Emblazoned across it, using my poetry magnets, was the following free-form ditty, which perplexed and angered me:

> *Beauty Style Whatever*
> *Drama is in the Hip*

"Drama is in the hip"? Who was doing this and why wouldn't they tell me? Why couldn't I get together with Doug—alone? Why was Kerrie turning into my nemesis? And how come it didn't matter that I finally felt pretty?

Little did I know that it would matter, a great deal, the very next day.

Chapter Eight

The next day, I went to Mass with Mom. Sometimes I don't get up in time for church, but that morning I was up before anyone else in the house. Anger does that to you. Turns you into an early riser. Connie and Tony, on the other hand, were sleeping in, or at least pretending to, so they didn't have to go through the lowered-eyes routine when Mom asked if they wanted to go to church with her.

I figured I needed all the help I could get, so I tagged along, wearing my khaki skirt and black tee again. And it was worth it. At least two people noticed how good I looked. One was old Mrs. Pompano, whose kids grew up with my grandparents. She squinted at me after church and said, "Is that Bianca? My, my, she has grown up so fast," which, in old person's speak, means "That bod's smokin'!"

The other was Richard Goldolfi, the choir director, who saw me after church and asked me to join the choir. While this might not seem like a compliment at first blush, you have to understand Goldofi. He's in his early twenties, just graduated from college, and is looking for a "little woman" big-time. He's been on more blind dates than, well, a blind person. His asking me to join the choir meant I was moving into the "eligible" category.

The real payoff, though, came that afternoon when Doug and I joined Sarah at the art gallery party. But let me back up a minute and share something strange.

When I got home from church, Connie told me Sarah had called.

Sarah had called on a Sunday morning? Early Sunday morning? Early Sunday morning wasn't chat-with-your-friends time. It was eat-cinnamon-buns-and-read-the-comics time. Or it was go-to-church-with-family time. If Sarah had called me this early, it was because something was wrong. Immediately, I thought it was another fight with Kerrie.

"She said she'd catch up with you later," Connie said when I tried to bump her off the computer to call back.

By the time "later" rolled around, I'd worked myself into what I'd call a "productive simmer." It was productive because I couldn't sit still, and so I finished a project for Music that wasn't due until Friday, got a head start on a book I needed to finish reading by Christmas break, did some cyber-shopping for Christmas gifts, painted my toenails and fingernails, and shortened a long black dress.

The black dress was originally long because we had to have black dresses or black pants for school chorus. Kerrie had given me a long black skirt she didn't like any more, and I used that for chorus now instead of my long black dress. So I actually hemmed the darn dress in about an hour and had a new addition to my wardrobe. It looked really good, too—just a plain sleeveless thing. So good, in fact, that I decided to wear it to the art gallery.

Normally, I'm not a dress person. I'm more of a slacks

or skirt person. But I was still so miffed about my day yesterday, and still wanting that "ooh-aah" payoff from Doug about my hair, that I decided I would overcome my dress phobia and look nice for a change. I paired the dress with dangling gold earrings and a thin gold chain my mom gave me last Christmas. After borrowing Connie's strappy sandals (she wouldn't miss them), I waited at the door for Doug so he wouldn't have to park.

When my mother saw me, she practically did a double-take.

"Bianca, you look very sophisticated!" But then she had to also throw in her usual "Mom" warning (every compliment is followed by a warning). "But you'll get cold. Take your jacket."

My jacket was not a jacket. It was a parka—no, make that an inflated balloon costume that made me look like the Michelin tire guy—and if you think I was going to put that over this black race-car of a dress, you're nuts. Heck, I've had buyer's remorse over that parka since the day after I bought it. My eye-rolling must have instantly communicated all this because Mom left the room and returned a few minutes later with a dark green pashmina shawl.

"Here," she said, handing it to me. "I was going to give it to you for Christmas, but it'll look so nice with that dress."

Before I had a chance to say more than a shocked "thanks!" Doug's blue Honda was inching into view, so I hopped on out, pulling the soft shawl around my shoulders.

Once in the car, I got my payoff. Doug looked at me for a full five seconds while someone honked behind him. Then he said, "You look great."

My bad mood evaporated.

In fact, after we got to the museum, my previous bad mood joined the Witness Protection Program. In my shortened black dress and new hair, I turned heads. Literally. As soon as we entered the building, a few folks by the door turned and looked my way. The ladies in the group scrunched their eyes up a millimeter, which I immediately recognized as envy-scrunch. Some blonde-pageboy woman came over with her hand extended. She was dressed in a black velvet pantsuit and plastic smile.

"Welcome. I'm Fawn Dexter. You must be Jean Connelly."

So this was Ms. Dexter of the flirtatious voice and mysterious secrets. She didn't look like the mastermind of any grand criminal plot.

Just then, Sarah came over. "No, she's not Jean Connelly. These are my friends you said it was okay to invite." Then she introduced us. Fawn looked disappointed. She hastily retracted her hand as if I had cooties, then just as quickly left us alone.

"Who's Jean Connelly and why does Fawn Dexter want to meet her?" I asked. Sarah popped a crab puff in her mouth and balled up the green napkin that had been holding it. She was wearing a neat navy skirt, white blouse, and clunky platform shoes.

"Fawn's my boss. Community and development director. Jean Connelly's some bigwig financier who's underwriting our next exhibit. Fawn's never met her but seen her picture." She looked over her shoulder. "Come on. I'll show you where the food is. Then I have to check in with Fawn to see if she needs me to do anything."

Sarah led us to a terrific spread of party food near the museum restaurant. A long table covered with a green cloth held silver platters of crab puffs, vegetables, and dip (and not just carrot slices—there were snow pea pods, scallions, cucumbers, and stuff I didn't even recognize), and a whole array of Japanese-style hors d'oeuvres, since this was an exhibit of Japanese prints. I passed on the sushi and went for the crab puffs. So did Doug.

"I heard you called," I said to Sarah, but she took a quick glance at Doug, immediately signaling to me that whatever she'd wanted to talk about was private.

"Doug, would you get me some of those strawberries down there?" I said, pointing to the far end of the table. While he moved away, Sarah whispered to me.

"Hector and I . . . went out on a date. He's an art student."

"So?"

"So that's why Fawn's so suspicious of him!" Sarah sounded exasperated. We only had a few seconds before Doug returned. I saw him standing in line by the strawberries. "She must think he can pull something off."

"You mean *forge* something."

She nodded her head.

"Did you ever talk to Fawn?" I asked. "You know, like I suggested."

"I tried," she said mournfully. "But I never could figure out how to do it. I managed to find out they'd hired your sister, though."

"Has Fawn mentioned Hector any more?" I already knew the answer to that one. Connie had told me they thought he was a good suspect.

"No. And I think that might be because she saw Hector and me talking."

"So she knows you're friends?"

"Yeah."

Doug was finished loading up a little plastic plate with berries, so we had to wrap this up fast.

"You really like Hector, don't you?"

"Yes."

"Then talk to him." Suddenly, I realized it was Hector who was the friend with "troubles"—the friend she'd IM'ed me about. "Tell him to come clean if he's done something wrong. Maybe it was just a prank."

"Okay."

Okay? That one word spoke volumes. She thought he *had* done something.

This whole conversation made me nervous. If Hector was involved, Sarah needed to stay far away from him. She wouldn't get many more second chances.

Doug returned and handed us plates. While he and I ate, Sarah disappeared to check in with Fawn. I was just beginning to enjoy myself again when a familiar voice greeted me.

"Bianca?"

It was Kerrie! She was there with her dad. Mr. Daniels smiled at Doug and me while Kerrie frowned. She was dressed in black pinstripe slacks and a black top. Black must be the color for exhibit openings. "What are *you* doing here?" Kerrie asked.

That wasn't the real question, though. The real question was, "why did you come to this opening without telling me, especially since it was Sarah who told you about it in the first place?" I was caught in the middle again.

"Uh, Sarah invited us. She said . . ."

Kerrie frowned in a melodramatic sort of way. "That's right. The interns got to invite two friends."

Mr. Daniels saw someone he knew and left Kerrie with Doug and me.

"How are things?" Doug asked her good-naturedly.

"Fine, I guess," she said.

Sarah returned a few seconds later. When she saw Kerrie, she visibly reddened. I felt like kicking her. She should have told Kerrie she'd invited me and Doug.

"What are *you* doing here?" Sarah asked Kerrie.

"My dad brought me. He's on the board, remember?" Kerrie said. "You didn't tell me you'd invited Bianca."

"I didn't have a chance," Sarah said. "You've been so busy lately."

"You're the one galavanting off to colleges."

"Well, I didn't galavant this weekend," Sarah said with an edge in her voice.

"It's not my fault your Boston trip got canceled."

"I didn't say it was," Sarah retorted. "But your dad did have to help you with your social studies project last week, which meant he had to catch up on work *this* weekend."

"Are you saying he shouldn't have?" Kerrie sounded like she was going to challenge Sarah to a duel. This was getting ridiculous. Time to step in and mediate again.

I moved in Kerrie and Sarah's direction at the same time I raised my hands in a "can't we all get along" kind of gesture that unfortunately collided with a huge silver tray of sushi being brought to the table by a tuxedoed server behind me.

The sushi tray then collided with Kerrie's black silk blouse. Sushi on silk—fashion fumble, big-time. Kerrie shrieked and her hands flailed in the air as if she'd been attacked by snakes. Come to think of it, some of that dead fish looked rather snake-like, so I don't blame her for screaming.

"I'm so sorry," I immediately said, grabbing gobs of green napkins and rubbing at her blouse. The waiter bent to pick up the tray while snarling "watch what you're doing" to me. Then Fawn came over and snarled at Sarah, except more politely.

"What's going on here?" she hissed, pushing her blonde hair behind an ear and looking with disgust at Kerrie.

"Uh, nothing. Just an accident, that's all, Miss Dexter," Sarah said.

While Sarah was trying to look helpful and innocent, Hector came over. "Can I help here?" he said, smiling at Sarah. And she smiled back. And blushed. We all felt the electricity in the air—electricity whose plug was promptly pulled by a very nervous Fawn Dexter.

"No! You should be doing your job. Walking the halls or something!" Dexter snapped. "Last thing we need is another . . ." Then she stopped herself and waved her hands in the air, which I interpreted to mean something like "just make this go away." She promptly made herself go away by walking toward someone coming through the door at that moment who had a haircut similar to mine. It must have been Jean Connelly.

Hector shrugged and pointed his finger at Sarah. "Later," he said. She smiled, but it was a troubled smile, and I knew whose troubles she was thinking about—his.

Kerrie, meanwhile, was not smiling. In fact, she was crying. Yes, crying. Her tears were dripping onto the sushi, returning those poor dead fish to their natural saltwater habitat. "Too late, Kerrie, it won't revive them," I wanted to scream. Instead, I added my consoling words to those already being offered by—you guessed it—Doug! He had his arm around her shoulder and was saying, "Ker, it's okay. Bianca didn't mean it."

Bianca didn't mean it? Did he think I deliberately sent that sushi missile her way?

Reinforcing this view was Kerrie herself. When her dad stepped over a few seconds later to ask what was the matter, she gulped out, "Bianca spilled a tray on me." In a heartbeat, I had gone from accidentally bumping into a waiter to purposely directing a food tray onto her fancy blouse. If I wasn't careful, Hector soon would be escorting me to the door for carrying a concealed deadly sushi tray.

I at least expected some sympathy from Sarah. But no, she chose this moment to get back in Kerrie's good graces.

"Come on, Ker, I'll take you to the office. I might have another blouse back there from when I changed after school this week."

Both Sarah and Doug escorted the sobbing Kerrie down the hallway while I was left holding a scrunched up gob of green paper napkins. After tossing it in a nearby trash bin, I looked ruefully at Mr. Daniels.

"It was an accident," I managed to murmur. "I wasn't even carrying the tray. Honest."

He gave me a quick artificial smile, put his hands in his pockets, and nodded. "She'll be fine. She's just a little sensitive right now." His gaze drifted to the door and his face brightened when an older man approached us, followed by a younger guy—a guy who looked like a blonde Hugh Grant. Same rakish smile and long face. Same perpetually-tousled hair. Same sparkling eyes.

I swooned. Well, not really. But swooning would certainly have felt better than skulking, which was what I felt like I was doing—skulking around after unintentionally causing my friend embarassment.

"Bertrand! Nice to see you," Mr. Daniels said, extending his hand to the older man. Then he turned to me. "Bianca Balducci, this is a fellow lawyer, Bertrand Witherspoon." Then, to Mr. Witherspoon, "Bianca is one of Kerrie and Sarah's best friends."

Witherspoon smiled at me and offered his hand. He smelled like nicotine—the musky aroma of a habitual smoker. After our introduction, he pointed to the Hugh Grant fellow. "This is my son, Neville. He's in town looking at Hopkins."

"How do you do?" Neville said, not taking his eyes off me. He spoke with a British accent, which just emphasized the Hugh Grant connection. Now I really did feel like swooning. *Tip for all men:* to impress women, speak with British accent.

Mr. Daniels started jabbering at Mr. Witherspoon about local politics, and it wasn't long before they drifted off, leaving me with the dashing Master Witherspoon ("Master" is what they call young men in Britain). Unlike Doug, who sported the traditional Dressy Clothes for a Guy—nice slacks, white shirt, and tie—Neville wore a sexily casual blue blazer, white shirt, and no tie. After his father departed the group, Neville grinned sheepishly, rolled his eyes, and ran his hand through his hair.

"Well, Miss Balducci, why don't you tell me about yourself? Do you work here?"

I laughed. Actually, my guffaw sounded more like seals barking, so I quickly stopped.

"No, no. I'm just a friend of someone who works here. Well, she doesn't really work here. She's doing an internship here, which I guess is like an apprenticeship. She's trying to get into college and it looks good on your resumé to do internships. But I'm not trying to get into college. I mean, not yet. I mean, I'm just a sophomore at St. John's." After that stunning demonstration of conversational skill, I paused and cleared my throat. "Where do you go to school, Neville?"

"Actually, nowhere at the present time. I graduated last spring, and I'm taking something of a hiatus after some school plans went pear-shaped on me, you see. Mummy wanted me to go to Oxford, but I wanted to travel a bit, so here I am."

Mummy? Hiatus? Oxford? Pear-shaped? Oh, baby, could he make the sweet talk.

He looked hungrily at the table of hors d'oeuvres. "I say, you Americans really know how to put on a party." He grabbed a crab puff and swallowed it in one ravenous gulp.

From around the corner, a bell rang and Fawn Dexter's high nasal voice could be heard urging people to join her in the lobby for a tour of the new exhibit.

Neville looked at me and smiled. "Would you do me the honor of escorting me, Miss Balducci?" He held out his arm as if I were a royal princess. What could I do? I didn't want to start a war or something! I placed my hand on his elbow.

"This should be fun," he said, winking at me. "We can hang back and I'll give you the real story on all these art works. My mother's an artist in London. There's a marvelous scandal brewing here, did you know?"

"I've only heard rumors," I said as he led me toward the back of the growing herd of people.

"It's quite the story. Some of their art works have been stolen. And replaced by brilliant fakes. It's quite rich." He laughed heartily just as Fawn Dexter started us all up a broad staircase.

Doug and Kerrie and Sarah were nowhere in sight. But at that point, I didn't much care. I'd hook up with them later—after Neville gave me a tour and filled me in on this "quite rich" scoop.

Chapter Nine

Fawn Dexter droned on about the humor and "whimsy" in the Japanese prints, Neville told me about the museum's scandal. I already knew most of it, but somehow it sounded fresh when told in a British accent. I kept saying "really?" and "wow" to each revelation, then had to remind myself I already knew that juicy bit of info. He told me about the "stolen" art, the fakes, the alarm, and how it was all "hush-hush" because the museum didn't want a scandal that would rock the confidence of patrons and contributors in the middle of a fundraising drive. He even mentioned how "some Mexican guard" was a prime suspect for the mess. The only new information I got out of Neville was who was at the other end of Fawn Dexter's flirty-voiced conversations. Turned out that Fawn and Bertrand—Neville's father—were an item.

"My sister Connie's on the case," I whispered to him. "She's a private investigator. I help her sometimes."

This elicited a broad grin from the dashing Master Witherspoon that had me headed into swoon territory once again.

He was a talented mimic and he sprinkled his story

with occasional lampoons of Miss Dexter as we observed the various prints from well behind the crowd.

"Doesn't this white space just speak to you?" He pointed to the background on one of the prints. "It's *decadent* yet spare, *shrill* yet muted, *hopeless* yet imbued with sunny optimism," he said, imitating the quick highs and lows of Miss Dexter's voice.

"Stop it, Neville. You're wicked!" I laughed. *Wicked?* Since when did I use the word "wicked" in conversation? Being around a Brit must have done that to me.

By this time, people were throwing us occasional looks that said our witty conversation was disturbing them, so I turned to a more serious topic.

"Who do you think is doing it and why?" I asked. "The phony art, I mean. Are they selling the originals?" And a more troubling thought occurred to me—what was Hector's role in all this? I saw him a few times as we made our way through the museum. And though Sarah liked him, I wondered if he wasn't taking advantage of her good nature, of her sympathy for the underdog. To me, Hector looked kind of shifty, with small squinty eyes and big, gangster-like shoulders.

"Selling them is hard to do, but not impossible. You could make a pretty penny if you knew the right markets. No, my guess is it's some frustrated artist effecting his own form of twisted revenge on an institution that has ignored his talents." He suddenly pointed to Hector, who stood with hands clasped in front of him in the corner of the room. "Did you know he's secretly an artist? Does wonderful watercolors that a couple centuries ago would have made him the toast of the town. Not so today. It's enough to drive a man to desperate measures."

"How do you know that?" I asked. A long shiver curled from my heels to the tip of my now-perfect hair.

Even Neville suspected Hector! I glanced at Hector again and studied him. Darn it, he could be getting Sarah into trouble. It wasn't fair. Sarah was too sweet. She needed to be protected.

"My father told me," Neville said, "and he heard it from Fawn."

The crowd started to move forward and Neville extended his arm once again.

"Would you do me the honor, mademoiselle?" he asked.

Remembering my Honors French, I said, "Mais oui, monsieur," which is about all I could say without sounding like I had a mouth full of marbles. It must have been enough, though, because he took and patted my hand and looped it over his arm, bending his head toward me as if we shared a secret.

"Don't look now, m'dear, but I think Hector is eyeing you rather suspiciously. You didn't, by any chance, slip a painting into your brassiere?" Then he looked at me with a wolf-like gaze that made me tremble and blush. "But of course you couldn't. Not the way that dress hugs you so deliciously."

I don't think I've ever been described as "delicious" before. And if some guy at school had just said that to me, I'd have swung at him. Or at least squinted. But somehow Neville could get away with saying a whole lot of things just because of his dreamy British accent. So when he pulled me a little closer, I didn't resist, and that's exactly how Doug found us—with Neville's arm slipped around my waist and his lips perilously close to my ear as he whispered sweet and funny nothings to me.

Doug was not amused. He stood ramrod straight, then shoved his hands in his pockets, looked at me, raised his eyebrows (which I was smart enough to know meant "what the hey is going on here?"), and pursed his lips before speaking.

"Kerrie's okay. Sarah's helping her. They said they'd wait for us downstairs."

Doug was jealous. And, I'm ashamed to admit, I liked it. Something inside me said, "Take that, you jerk. You ignored me to take care of sob sister Kerrie, so this is what you get—your girlfriend on the arms of Hugh Grant."

But once I'd had my satisfying moment of silent revenge, I pulled away from Neville and stood next to Doug. I might be weak, but I'm not stupid. Doug was my guy.

And Doug wasn't stupid, either. He knew Neville was putting the moves on me. Staking his claim, Doug grabbed my hand.

"Let's catch up with the crowd," he said as if actually interested in the art exhibit. I was touched. Doug was pretending to like this hoity-toity stuff just to please me. My eyes welled with tears of joy.

Well, not really. But my mouth turned up in a kind of goofy grin that I'm sure knocked out my sophisticated look, good haircut or not.

Neville, meanwhile, was undaunted by Doug's territorial attitude. He strode right along with us, as if we were the Three Musketeers. And he kept up his funny banter, which annoyed Doug as well as most of the other art patrons within earshot.

Trouble is, I'm a sucker for amusing banter. Okay, okay, I'm a sucker for anything silly—it doesn't even need to rise to the level of "banter." So I had a hard time controlling myself. To keep from laughing, I kept biting the insides of my cheeks. If this kept up much longer, I was going to need oral surgery by the time we were finished.

But we were finished in a few minutes. Fawn Dexter said something about the generosity of several important patrons such as Jean Connelly, everyone applauded, and we were on our way back to the food again.

When we tramped back downstairs, Kerrie and Sarah were waiting for us, looking like the best of friends, which is what they used to be. In fact, it now looked like Kerrie was comforting Sarah, who was pale and distracted, glancing this way and that as if looking for someone. Spotting Hector across the room, she shot him a glance that said "betrayal." He, meanwhile, looked at her like a confused puppy, which, come to think of it, is a look I've seen on a lot of guys' faces. It must be standard issue.

I did the introductions and then turned to Sarah.

"You look like you've seen a ghost."

"Well, I . . ."

Kerrie stepped forward. "She thought she was locked out."

"I had to go to my car," Sarah said. "I had a blouse there. And when I tried to get back in, the door was locked."

I looked over my shoulder at the museum's front door, which was open.

"Not that door," Sarah said. "The one by the dumpster."

Hector headed our way, and behind him I saw another figure enter the scene, a very familiar figure. Connie! But she didn't come toward us—I'm not even sure she noticed me or cared that I was there. Instead, she headed purposefully up the stairs as if on a mission.

Sarah saw her, too, and quickly turned to us to announce she was hungry. It was as if she wanted to draw attention away from Connie's presence.

"I can drive us all somewhere. Who wants to go?" she asked with false bravado.

"Sounds smashing," Neville said. "You'll go, won't you, Bianca?"

Whoa, Neville. Suddenly he was part of our group. Grimacing, Doug squeezed my hand tighter. "I have my own car. But I have a term paper due . . ." Doug said.

Neville grinned devilishly. "Then Bianca can come with us while you scoot on home to Mummy."

This didn't sit too well with Doug. I actually saw the muscles in his jaw working as he struggled to control his anger. I was reminded of those nature shows where two rams buck at each other, horns intertwining.

"I'm tired anyway," I said lamely, wanting to avoid any carnage.

"Aw, come on, Bianc, it'll be fun," said Kerrie. "We haven't done anything together in a long time." She was right. We hadn't done anything together in a long time because of the unspoken feud between her and Sarah. This was reconciliation time and I didn't want to miss it. Besides, I might be needed for more mediation.

"Yes, Bianca, it *will* be fun," said Neville. "Where are you going? One of those chain places, I hope. Where there are plastic menus and food that's the same the whole country over." He smiled and rocked on his heels. "I love those places."

While Neville launched into a funny riff on things he liked about America, I caught sight of Hector talking quietly to Sarah, just on the edge of our group. I edged a little closer to eavesdrop.

"I thought we were going out together," Hector was saying. He sounded miffed.

"Not tonight," she whispered back.

"I get it—*your* friends. I don't swim in the same sea."

He turned his back and walked away. Sarah stared after him but came back to our group.

". . . and we watch 'ER,' 'Friends,' 'Frasier'—American shows are very popular at home. And music, too. Eminem is well good, if you ask me," Neville was saying.

" 'Well good'?" Kerrie asked. "Don't you mean 'very'?"

"I suppose," Neville laughed. "It's how we say things. Like a *bird*. If she's what you call 'hot,' she's 'well fit' in Britain." Neville looked straight at me and I blushed.

"A bird?" Kerrie chirped.

"A girl," I explained. I might not have the slang dictionary, but I was good at getting things from context. And this context was getting too "well fit" for me.

"Let's go," I said brightly.

"We could go to Applebee's," Sarah said to us, her voice trembling. "They have fajitas."

"I love Mexican food. Oh, let's do go," Neville chimed in.

Doug looked at me, then at Neville, and must have made an instant calculation. "I can go for a little while. We'll meet you there."

"Just a sec. I need to go to the ladies room," I said, and rushed off looking for Connie.

I didn't find Connie, but I did find Hector. When I came upon him just around the corner from the crowd, he was locking up a closet with a big ring of keys.

"Hector," I blurted out, "I understand you're an art student."

He looked surprised and nodded slowly. "Yeah. So?"

"What kind of stuff do you do?" I tried to sound conversational, but I knew I was coming off as just weird. Heck, I felt weird.

"Watercolors. Nothing like this." He swept his arm around in a gesture that included the whole museum, but I knew what he meant. Hector's art was probably not what galleries and museums were looking for. Maybe Hector *was* behind all the museum shenanigans, and maybe that's why Sarah was worried. And darn it, she couldn't afford to get into trouble even if she was moony over a sweet-looking art student who moonlighted as a guard. I'd learned my lesson with Sarah already—don't be quiet when you think something bad is on the horizon. So, pardon the pun, but I forged ahead. She might not have the courage to.

"Look, Hector," I said, wagging my finger at him. "Sarah is one of my best friends and I don't want her getting hurt. A month or so ago, she was in big trouble, and if she even gets near that kind of trouble again—with the law and all—she won't get any breaks. And I happen to know that the museum has been missing a few things and Sarah is afraid her friend has done something wrong, so all I can say is—stay away from her, buster, until you straighten up and fly right!"

Woohoo—what a lecture! Now I understand why grown-ups enjoy it so much. The rush of power, the thrill of control, the high of being The Authority. It's a wonder they don't indulge in it more often.

But if I'd expected Hector to simper and cower, beg for forgiveness, and back away, I was sorely mistaken. Instead, he pulled himself up like a bear ready to strike, and he unleashed his own lecture. Except it wasn't really a lecture. It was the truth. And the reason I know it was the truth is because the truth has this funny way of zooming in on you like a heat-seeking missile. It doesn't miss.

"You can tell Sarah she has nothing to worry about," he hissed and stomped off.

In those ten words, he had communicated an essay's worth of info. He was not the thief. And he was not going to pursue a woman—Sarah—who thought he was.

Way to go, Bianca. I'd just managed, at one and the same time, to falsely accuse a man I didn't even know, and to ruin my best friend's budding romance with him. Was I talented or what?

Chapter Ten

The car ride to Applebee's was silent and slow. I was in my own world, trying to figure out how to break it to Sarah that I'd ruined her relationship with Hector, while also berating myself for zeroing in on him in the first place. But hey, Sarah herself had been concerned about him, so I wasn't completely in left field on this. I just was missing too much information. I had to talk to Connie. I started choosing the various torture methods I could use to pry the info out of her that night. Perhaps I'd remove all the tofu from the house and substitute packages of Jimmy Dean's breakfast sausage.

My silent musings soon gave way to silent fuming, however, when I realized that Doug was engaging in his own fume fest. Why should he enjoy it alone, right?

Doug always drives slowly, which is okay by me. I'd rather have that than some Dale Earnhardt wannabe behind the wheel. But today, his slowness was matched by a clenched jaw version of simmering irritation, which just lit my own irk-fuse, if you know what I mean.

Okay, question for guys now: Why can't you just come out and say what's on your mind? I mean, with girls, it's blah, blah, blah, blah, blah, blah, blah. A guy would have to be an alien mutant not to know what's on a girl's mind. (Come to think of it, maybe guys *are* mutants.)

But guys, I have discovered, are real Silent Sams. Something bothers them, they mope and fume, but don't say a word. Then, like some big loping dog, they eventually get over it or snarl and bark at you.

Now, I knew that Doug was miffed because of the whole Neville thing. I was miffed that he was miffed because I had been miffed about the Kerrie thing, but I had not moped and fumed. So he shouldn't either, right? Keep it to himself!

Uh-oh. He *was* keeping it to himself. That was the problem! I needed to rethink this whole comeuppance flirting thing.

"It's nice that Kerrie and Sarah are getting along again, isn't it?" I asked, looking over at him.

"Yup," he said, keeping his eyes on the road.

That was the sum total of our pre-Applebee's conversation. Every time I thought of something else to say, traffic picked up and I didn't want to distract him.

By the time Doug and I finally arrived at the restaurant, Neville had Sarah and Kerrie laughing hysterically with his imitations of Fawn Dexter, and they'd long ago placed their order of fried onion strips. Doug and I joined them at the round table, but as Neville stood, he held out a chair for me next to him instead of the one I was heading for next to Kerrie. What's a girl to do?

As I settled between Doug and Neville, I thought I heard Doug growl.

Well, not really. But he didn't look too happy, which kind of set the tone for the rest of our meal. Sarah had clearly put her troubles with Hector behind her, which was a good thing since she didn't know I'd caused more trouble ahead. I'd have some explaining to do, and I wanted to catch her alone before she left the restaurant so I could do my guilt-dump and get it over with.

But maybe Hector *was* guilty of something, if only a "prank." I couldn't tell! I was confused.

Confusion, though, gave way in short order to fun because it turned out that Neville was a hoot. When I sat down, he was just ordering "a brew" from a startled waitress.

"I'm going to have to card you," the woman said to him, peering over half-glasses.

"What?" Neville looked perplexed and disgusted.

"She means she needs to see identification to know how old you are," Kerrie explained.

"What's my age got to do with it?" Neville asked.

"You can't drink alcohol unless you're twenty-one," Doug chimed in, his tone of voice conveying his belief that Neville was pretty dumb for not knowing this.

"Alcohol? Since when does tea have alcohol in it?" Neville said.

So that's when we learned that tea is "a brew" in England, as in "after the soap on TV, I'll fix myself a brew." Now, I suspect Neville knew a brew wasn't a brew here in the old US of A, but it certainly set us up for another round of fascinating chitchat on the differences between our slang and our outlook on each other.

According to Neville, most of his countrymen think all Americans carry guns just like John Wayne. And even though he didn't need to show ID for his "brew" of tea, he found it pretty annoying that he couldn't drink here, because in Britain, he could drink at age eighteen.

When our food arrived, he treated us to yet more instruction.

"These," he said, holding up a French fry, "are chips."

"Well, what are chips then? I mean potato chips?" Sarah asked.

"Crisps," he answered, popping a fry into his mouth.

"What about chocolate chips?" Doug asked smugly in an "ah-ha, gotcha" kind of voice.

"Hmm . . . those things in cookies? Well the cookies are just chocolate chip cookies. But other cookies, like macaroons and such, are biscuits," Neville answered, smiling. Doug just frowned.

Poor Doug. No, poor me! I'd put up with days of silent jealousy during his sympathy fest with Kerrie. Now that I was soaking up some attention, he was being Mr. Jealous Boyfriend.

Was that good or bad? I didn't know! The hottie in me said, "Go, girl, let him seethe!" But the Good Teen in me said, "Now, now, Bianc, show some sympathy for the lovesick puppy." I was going to have to start wearing an aluminum hat to block these inner voices!

As we ate, Kerrie and Sarah produced a veritable on-slaught of chatter. They were either making up for lost time or putting on a Public Display of Reconciliation for all of us to admire. Whatever, it was a good thing they were such motormouths because Doug was absolutely mum.

Okay, okay, I don't usually say "mum," but with Neville around, my thoughts were coming through with a British accent. How do I turn this thing off?

It didn't help matters that Neville spoke to me a lot, asking me what I thought about the exhibit, what I liked about my school, what kind of music I listened to. It was clear he liked me, and Doug was picking up the vibes.

All of this made me a little angry because, though I enjoyed the attention, I found myself holding back so as not to upset Doug, which just made me resentful of

Doug. Not a good set of feelings to have toward your boyfriend.

By the time we finished our dinners, I was a simmering stew pot of mixed feelings. Doug's attitude held me back from having fun. I'd not only missed out on enjoying Neville's attention, the whole meal at Applebee's had been spoiled, too, because Doug more than once mentioned he had a big paper to work on and he needed to get going.

You have to understand. I love chain restaurants—fast food or slow food. McDonald's, Wendy's, Applebee's, Olive Garden, Red Lobster—they're all high on my list of guilty pleasures. But I hadn't been allowed to savor this Applebee's moment because my boyfriend was dragging me down.

So, when we got ready to leave and Neville oh so casually said, "I'd love for someone to show me around Baltimore. Since you have to run off, Doug, why don't I let Bianca be my guide?" I was primed.

Doug just stood there and sputtered. Well, maybe not exactly sputtered. But he did say, "Uh, well, um . . ." and gritted his teeth. Then he said something that pushed me ever closer to Neville's arms. He said, "Bianca's, uh, got to study, too."

He might as well have spray painted "Stupid Girl" on my forehead. But even this wasn't enough to tip me over the edge completely. No, it was when I protested. When I said, "I don't need to study, I—"

"Didn't you tell me you got a bad grade in history?" he interrupted.

My face reddened. I didn't get a bad grade in history! I just got a B when I wanted an A, and that was only because my paper was a day late, and even *that* wasn't my fault! Now he was making me look like a cultural Neanderthal around this sophisticated British guy. And as we know, British guys (and girls) don't need to be taught history because they are hard-wired to know it.

"I don't need to study," I said. Now I was the one with gritted teeth. Quick, call an orthodontist before we both mangle our perfect pearly whites. "So I can go with you, Neville."

I smiled at Doug. "I wouldn't want Neville to think we're not good hosts," I said, as if I was part of the official United States Welcome Wagon.

I expected Kerrie and Sarah to pipe up at this point and offer to come, too, and I looked at them, but they didn't pick up the brain signals I was beaming their way. They both started sympathizing with Doug's need to study, talking about papers due and homework undone.

Neville impressed us all by paying the bill. Doug left with Sarah and Kerrie. I stood at the counter as Neville waited for change. And you know what? I didn't even want to go with him any more! I wanted to go home. No, let me be more specific—I wanted my boyfriend to drive me home in that slow, crazy way of his, and I wanted him to walk me to my door and say sweet things to me like "Uh, see ya tomorrow, I guess." I also wanted to dream about the Mistletoe Dance and pepper Connie with questions about the museum shenanigans.

But no, I had to prove just what an independent woman I was—hear me roar—so I had to leave Doug in the dust. Watching my boyfriend and two best friends make their way to the parking lot, I had the certain sense that I'd made a big mistake.

Chapter Eleven

Boy, was it ever! A big mistake, that is. As soon as I got in Neville's car, I regretted it. He was driving his father's silver Mercedes, a car with a lot of power and speed. And whereas Doug was Mr. Cautious behind the wheel (to the extreme), Neville was devil-may-care. He careened down boulevards, squealed around corners, and screeched to a halt behind stopped trucks with so little room to spare that I saw my life flashing before my eyes on more than one occasion. Add to this his admitted "need to get used to this right side of the road thing," and you had a recipe for disaster.

So, after a quick turn around the Harbor, where I pointed out things of interest in a thin, high-pitched voice, I pretended to not really know where most things were (Fort McHenry? Must be in Washington!), and asked him to take me home, the location of which I absolutely knew.

As we neared the final dropoff, it was getting dark. Neville double-parked in front of my house, but before I could say "thanks for the near-death experience" and scoot out, he was bounding around to open my door and escort me to the door.

Once there, he told me he'd like to see me again. And he kissed me goodnight.

As soon as I saw what he was up to, I pulled away, but it was too late. He grabbed my arm and planted a wet one on me in the blink of an eye. Not that I did blink. I had my eyes wide open.

Now, I'm not going to lie to you and say that being kissed by a suave, good-looking Brit is some kind of hardship. And come on—even the most loyal of girl-friends can fantasize about a super hunk or two. If Doug hadn't been so paranoid about Neville to begin with, I'd probably have laughed off the kiss as a friendly gesture best not repeated.

But instead, I felt guilty. And what do we do when we feel guilty? All together now—we confess!

After I slammed the door shut and said hi to Mom, who was at the kitchen table sipping a cup of tea and doing the Sunday crossword puzzle, I headed to the computer.

"Can I get online?" I asked.

"Huh? Sure," Mom said. "Did you have a good time?"

"Yup. Great," I said. But I was already clicking through to my e-mail box. Nothing there except a few Viagra ads, but I could see that Kerrie was already online, so I IMed her right away.

"you're home early," she wrote back after my hello.

"didn't like being out alone," I responded. "how was doug?"

"fine. he left right when we did. haven't talked to him."

Hmm . . . didn't like that. It implied that she did talk to him on other occasions.

"have fun with Neville?" she asked.

"it was okay." Then, the confession: "he kissed me good night, can you believe it?"

"you're kidding."

"i think he likes me."

"watch out for him."

"don't worry. i'm doug's girl."

"glad to hear that. doug's a great guy."

For some reason, this last message irked me. It implied a familiarity I didn't care for—"don't go breaking Doug's heart because I, Kerrie, am his guardian angel, and he's been great to you."

But all I wrote back was "i know. what are you doing?"

Then she started telling me about how she just finished her English paper and Sarah was talking to her dad about colleges. It made me feel good to know they were on an even keel again, even if my life was a busted dinghy in *The Perfect Storm*.

Okay, I know what you're thinking about now. You're thinking, why did I blurt out that Neville had kissed me? But I felt unguilted as soon as I did it. It made the whole incident feel normal, run-of-the-mill. "Oh, by the way, Neville kissed me." That sort of thing. It put it in perspective.

Just as I was about to log off, something odd happened. Sarah chimed in, using Kerrie's IM screen name.

"sarah here. give me a call," she typed.

Uh-oh. She must have found out how I'd ruined her budding romance with Hector. That'll be a fun phone conversation, I figured. Before I was able to type a response, though, she sent another message my way.

"is connie home?" she wrote.

Egads. Why was she asking that? I felt like screaming.

As if on cue, Connie wandered into the kitchen just then with the cordless in hand, and sweetly asked me if I'd free up the phone line.

"Haven't you been on there long enough?" she said in her usual dulcet tones.

"I just got on."

Connie turned to Mom for reinforcement. "How long's she been on?"

Because she didn't answer right away, I could tell that Mom hadn't been paying attention to the time. It didn't matter, though. She took Connie's side all the same.

"Let your sister use the phone, Bianca," she said.

With a loving grimace in Connie's direction, I typed a quick "g2g, connie's here—needs to use phone," said my good-byes to Sarah and Kerrie, and exited the e-mail program.

Connie immediately punched the phone's "on" button, clicked off, and dialed the seven-digit voice mail retrieval system. As she listened to the recording, she smiled wickedly at me, which meant it was a message for me.

"Hey, let me listen!" I said, reaching for the phone.

"Be quick! I need to make a call."

No wonder she was smirking. It was debonair Neville, calling from his father's cell phone on the way home, telling me what a really "fine time" he'd had and how he hoped he could call me sometime soon.

"I thought you had a boyfriend," Connie said when I handed her back the phone.

Mom looked up again, puzzled and concerned. "What?"

"I do have a boyfriend. Neville's just a . . . friend. Someone I just met."

"Who's Neville?" Mom asked.

"Someone I met at the art exhibit. Neville Witherspoon. The son of one of the museum directors."

"Neville *Witherspoon?*" Connie asked, her eyes wide as saucers. "As in *the* Witherspoons?"

"Yeah, that's the one. Why?"

"I've been trying to get in to see the elder Mr. Witherspoon for months," she said. "His law firm keeps a PI on retainer. I've been wanting to do a presentation but can't get my foot in the door."

My mother looked at me and I instantly knew what she was thinking: maybe you can help out your sister, hon.

"I hardly know him!" I practically shouted. Yup. But he did kiss me good night. "And besides, I have a boyfriend."

"Boyfriend or not, if you see Neville again, tell him about me, would you? Maybe mention that I've been trying to see his father."

I got up and started to leave the room, but Connie continued talking after me. "Ask him if there's anyone in particular I should ask to see!"

On the stairs, I turned to her and smiled. Now was my chance to cash in. I've found you can't put sibling-capital in the bank. You can only spend it when you get it. So, if your sibling wants something from you, use up the goodwill payment early.

"Let me use the phone first," I said sweetly.

"What?"

"I've got to call Sarah quick. She said she needs to talk to me. And maybe to you, too," I said, reaching for the phone from Connie's hand. She didn't resist.

As I ran upstairs to my room, I punched in the Daniels' phone number. Sarah answered on the second ring, which meant she'd been hoping I'd call her.

"What's up?" I asked nonchalantly.

"I've got a big problem!" she whispered. "Hold on."

I could hear her walking, and knew she was probably

headed for a private spot in the house where no one would overhear. I was in my room by now and closed the door so the cone of silence could descend over both of us.

"I . . . I found something," she said breathlessly after a few seconds.

"Found what?"

In the background, I heard Mrs. Daniels' voice saying something about carry-out for dinner tomorrow night. I love carry-out.

"Can I come over?" Sarah asked. "I'll show you."

I thought about the little bit of homework I'd yet to do. I thought about the hem on my uniform skirt I had to fix. I thought about the call to Doug I wanted to make. And I sighed.

"Sure," I said. "Connie's here, too."

"Good." After she hung up, I sat for a minute with the phone in my hands, wondering what I was getting myself into.

Twenty minutes later, Sarah was knocking at the door. But when I went to ask her in, she shook her head "no" and asked me to come outside with her.

"Maybe I should get Connie," I offered, remembering her request to talk to my sister. I didn't want to get in over my head. I'd done enough of that already.

Quickly, I two-at-a-timed the steps upstairs and barged into Connie's room without knocking. She was still on the phone from when I handed over the cordless fifteen minutes earlier. From the sappy smile on her face, I could tell it wasn't a business call.

"Tell Kurt you have to go," I said. "I need you. Business." I rushed back out before she had a chance to ask questions, but saw anger clouds storm onto her face. I figured the Witherspoon connection was enough to entice her. She might assume I had Neville by the ear, waiting to hear her sales pitch.

Shortly after I landed outside on the top marble step, Connie joined us. If she was disappointed the Witherspoon firm wasn't there waiting for her, she didn't let it show.

"What's up?" she asked, thumping her hands against her arms to warm up. It was getting a bit nippy.

Sarah looked at both of us with wide, scared eyes. "Come with me."

We followed her down the street to where her old beat-up car was parked, its front fenders the only two inches of the car safely inside the "No Parking Beyond This Sign" sign. Looking up and down the street both ways to make sure no one saw her, she went to the trunk, which she smacked hard with her fist. It popped open. (Some old-fashioned automatic opener, I guess.)

Inside, on top of some old newspapers, a tire, a flashlight, a battered case of some kind, and two *Cosmopolitan* magazines, was a painting. It was blue and white and gray, kind of streaky, with a yellow ball the size of a quarter painted in the upper right hand corner. Outside of the museum, it didn't look like art any more. It looked like a child's imagination gone wild, kind of whimsical and playful, and if it hadn't been on stretched canvas, I could have seen it smiling from some proud mom's refrigerator door, anchored by magnets from the local appliance repair shop.

"Holy sh—" Connie began to say, but I trumped her with my own shriek of "Sarah! How on earth did you get this?"

Her eyes teared up, and she shook her head and shrugged her shoulders. "I don't know! I don't know! It was there when I went to get my blouse out of my car, when I was trying to find a blouse Kerrie could change into at the museum!"

Oh, man! That was when she couldn't get back in because the car door had been locked. Whoever put it in her trunk had keys. Probably Hector!

Connie leaned over and studied it. "This is it," she said definitively. "I'd put money on it."

"This is *what?*" I asked.

"The painting that went missing this weekend."

"There weren't any missing paintings that I saw," I said. Yup, like the museum would just let an empty frame hang on the wall as an advertisement for would-be art thieves ("Steal from us! We won't notice!")

"A Bargenstahler," she said, accent and all. "Some up-and-coming German. Worth about twenty grand or more. And if he gets hot, it could be worth lots more in a few years." She must have been studying art appraisals.

"When was it taken?" I asked.

"They're not sure. A replacement was hung in its place, but no one noticed until this weekend."

"You mean a forgery was put up?" I pressed. Sarah stood mute and afraid in the cold dark evening.

"Yup," said Connie, who turned the moment she heard a car drive up behind us, and quickly slammed the trunk so no one would see the painting.

Then Connie pulled a Polaroid photo from the breast pocket of her blue Oxford shirt. She held it out for us to see. Although it was cheesy, it appeared to be a picture of a painting about the same size as the Bargenstahler, and in the same shades. But the streaks in the Polaroid's painting were at a sharper angle. And the yellow ball was muddy, as if the painter hadn't bothered to clean his brush before dipping it in the new color.

"Whoever did that fake isn't very good," I murmured.

Connie laughed. "That's the beauty of this scheme. Whoever's taking these things only takes abstracts and doesn't even bother to do a full-court-press forgery. He just uses whatever paint's on hand and throws it on the same-sized canvas in the same general shapes." She tapped her nail on the photo. "That's standard-issue gray paint from Home Depot."

"What am I going to do?" asked Sarah. "I can't just take this to the police! I didn't even know what it was at first!" She sounded like she was going to cry.

Connie's head snapped up. "What do you mean, *at first?*" Connie said. "Who'd you talk to? How'd you find out?"

"I called someone," Sarah said sheepishly.

"Hector!" I said. "Oh no!"

"The guard?" Connie asked. Can we all say "Deep doo-doo"?

Sarah nodded.

"You called Hector?" Connie shook her head in amazement and didn't wait for an answer. "Okay, here's what I'm going to do. I'm going to call Fawn at the museum and tell her I've got the Bargenstahler and will drop it off tonight. Wait right here."

She ran back to the house while Sarah and I stood out in the cold.

"Sarah," I said, "why'd you call Hector?"

"Because I thought I was in trouble. I needed help." She rubbed her cold arms. "And he's innocent!"

But she sounded like she was still convincing herself of that point. She called Hector, I guessed, because she wanted to reassure herself that he wasn't guilty. Whatever he'd said, it hadn't quite done the trick. She still had doubts. And so did I.

Finding the Forger

In a minute, Connie was back with her car keys and two sweaters, one for each of us.

"Come on," Connie said. "We're going for a milk-shake. I want to talk."

I had a strong feeling that the talk would have to take priority over the milkshake.

Chapter Twelve

Shakey's Olde Fashioned Soda Shoppe, a new corner store just two blocks from home, was designed as a cheery little spot, what with its white-and-black tile and wrought iron chairs and tables. Tonight, however, as Connie laid it on the line, a cloud of gloom hovered over our table by the door.

After gathering information from Sarah—when had she last looked in her trunk, where had the car been parked at the museum, who had keys to that door, and what did Sarah know about Hector—Connie set it all out for her, cold and hard.

"Hector's the obvious suspect," Connie said, staring at Sarah. Sarah's fingers played with the bottom of her milkshake glass. "He had the smarts, the know-how," Connie continued. "And he probably knew your trunk would pop open." She sipped at her kiwi smoothie.

"But why would he put it in my trunk?"

"To throw people off the trail. If they suspect you, the heat's off him," said Connie.

"Hector wouldn't do that to me!" protested Sarah, whose milkshake was hardly touched, whereas mine was already gone. She reached over and grabbed Connie's hand. "You're not going to turn him in, are you?"

"It isn't my job to turn him in," Connie said, matter-of-factly. "It's my job just to tell my client what I've found out and the conclusions I've drawn from it."

Well, that was hardly fair. We all knew what conclusions she was drawing.

"When will you be doing this telling?" I asked Connie, squinting my eyes at her to send the message I was on Sarah's side in this fight.

"Probably tonight."

"Tonight?" Sarah pulled back from the table.

"You can't be running around town with that stolen painting in your car, Sarah," Connie said to her. "It has to go back."

Sarah slumped in her seat and sighed heavily. She looked down at her nail-bitten fingers, twisted her mouth to one side, and looked up suddenly. "Why can't we just replace it?"

"What?!" Connie and I said in unison. Neither of us said what we were both thinking—that Sarah's desire to make things right meant she also thought Hector was responsible.

But maybe Connie wasn't thinking that exactly. She leaned into the table and looked intently at Sarah. "If you helped a friend because you thought it would keep him out of trouble, but you weren't part of the original trouble, that isn't as bad as being responsible for the trouble itself."

Okay, I can be dense sometimes, but when it comes to understanding my sister, I'm practically a member of sibling-Mensa. Her compassionate little speech meant only one thing—she thought Sarah was in on it! It was bad enough Hector had betrayed Sarah. Now Connie was piling on the guilty verdict, too.

"Lay off, Connie!" I said. "Sarah didn't do anything wrong. She told you—she found it in her car."

Connie was silent. I tried to stare at her, but the daggers in my eyes didn't fire.

"I didn't help anybody do anything wrong!" Sarah said with the indignation of the unfairly accused. "And neither did Hector." She looked around her as if trying to decide whether to bolt. "And . . . and there's an easy enough way to prove it. The security camera tapes. Have you looked at them?"

Connie slumped back in her seat. Sarah had hit on something.

"Just got 'em. But they've been looked over already."

"What about the ones from today?" Sarah asked defiantly.

"I can pick them up tomorrow."

"That sounds like a good idea, Connie," I said. "If Hector put the painting in Sarah's car, it would show up on a security tape—at least it'd show him walking down that corridor with the painting."

"All right."

Connie's "all right" inspired me. I pressed forward. "It's getting kind of late. If you're so concerned about your client, shouldn't you be getting the painting back to her instead of jawboning with us?" Yes, I actually said "jawboning." I thought it sounded, oh, I don't know, kind of detective-like.

"You're right," said Connie. She reached in her jeans pocket and pulled out a few bills, which she threw on the table like the private investigator she was. Then we all stood and made our way to the door.

Connie drove us home in silence and easily maneuvered into a just-her-car's-size parking spot not too far from Sarah's car.

We got out and stood shivering while Sarah went to her car to retrieve the painting.

"You know," said Connie, watching Sarah thwump the trunk to open it, "I probably should have—"

"Ohmygod!" Sarah shrieked as the trunk lid popped open. We rushed to see what was the matter. I was thinking "snake!"

Well, just for a nanosecond. Then my real brain kicked in and I mentally finished the sentence that Connie had started—that she should have immediately taken possession of the painting instead of leaving it in Sarah's car, because . . .

"It's gone!" Connie stomped her foot and cursed as she looked into the trunk. "And I just called them and told them I had it!" She smacked her head with her hand. "Why couldn't I have waited? Why? Why? Why?"

That's what I love about my sister. Like me, she makes mistakes.

She ran out into the middle of the street, looking up and down as if she'd actually see some thief running high-kneed down the asphalt with the painting. She groaned and let loose a cascade of expletives, then looked at us and said "sorry" as if we hadn't heard those words before. (Had she forgotten what high school is like?)

Pulling a pair of tight leather gloves from her pocket, she quickly put them on and rushed back to the trunk, where she rummaged through the mess that was left.

"Nothing else was taken," she said more to herself than to us.

"Well, there wasn't much else but junk," I volunteered.

"There was this!" Connie dragged out a heavy case.

"My laptop," Sarah said mournfully.

"You have a laptop?" I asked. I had to share one computer with two siblings, but Sarah had her own laptop? I was getting farther and farther behind in the keeping-up-with-the-Joneses race.

"It's an old one. Mr. Daniels lets me use it. I put it in the trunk because I didn't want it sitting out in the open where someone could see it."

"And steal it," Connie added. "But they didn't steal it. They only took the painting."

"They were looking for the painting," I said in a low voice. A shiver coursed up my spine. Someone had followed Sarah. I turned to her. "Who knew you were coming here?"

"I don't know!" She looked like she was going to cry. "You. Kerrie."

"What did you tell Kerrie?" I asked.

"That I had something to talk to you about."

Great! Now Kerrie would be back in her jealous mode.

"Anybody else know where you were?" Connie pressed.

Sarah silently shook her head. While Sarah thought, Connie pulled out her cell phone and handed it to Sarah.

"Call Kerrie and ask if anyone called, asking where you were," Connie told her.

While Sarah punched in the numbers and did as she was told, Mom appeared on the front steps.

"Why don't you girls come inside? It's getting cold out there."

"We'll be in in a sec," I said cheerily. "We're just making some plans."

"I can make hot chocolate," Mom offered.

"No thanks!" I said, so perky that I'm sure I was not only busting the perkometer scale, but practically achieving spontaneous combustion. It was enough to do the trick. Mom closed the door and left us alone. By this time, Sarah was off the phone and clearly uncomfortable.

"Well?" Connie asked.

"Hector called," she said sadly.

Chapter Thirteen

After Sarah went home, Connie and I talked for about a half hour out there on the cold street.

"It doesn't look good for Hector," she said, holding her cell phone. I knew what that meant. She was going to call An Authority (either Fawn Dexter or the police) and divulge all—finding the painting in Sarah's trunk, finding it stolen again, finding out that Hector knew where Sarah was.

"You can't," I argued preemptively. "You know they'll think Sarah did something wrong, too."

Connie pressed her lips together and folded her arms over her chest.

"You know," she said, squinting at me, "sometimes people used to being in trouble have a hard time giving up trouble."

"What?!"

"The lines get blurred. And they never get them straight again."

"Are you talking about art or about Sarah?" I asked sarcastically.

She harrumphed, which is Balducci for "you know what I mean."

"I have to tell," she continued. "I can't hide what I know."

"Wait a minute," I said, putting my hands on my hips. Oh yes, I put my hands on my hips. There are some gestures that never go out of style. "You don't usually tell clients everything until you solve the case. You just want to give up the info on Sarah and Hector to cover your butt for losing the painting!"

"I did not lose the painting. I never had the painting. Sarah had the painting." But her tone sent a different message. It said "Yes, I lost the painting and I'm toast if they blame me."

"But once you found the painting, you should have taken custody of it," I said in that charming *neener-neener-neener* tone known to siblings everywhere. "Immediately."

"I did have custody of it—in Sarah's car." Connie's voice sounded high and squeaky, which meant I was hitting a bull's-eye. The only reason she would hand over Sarah and Hector now, without corroborating information, was because it would make her look less foolish.

"And it won't help, anyway," I said. "You know they're going to get mad at you no matter who you betray."

"I'm not betraying anybody, Bianca! You're too much! Where do you get this stuff?" she said, flailing her arms in the air, and dropping her cell phone. I scrambled for it and held it tight to my chest.

"Give it over," she seethed.

"On one condition."

"Are you nuts? What condition?"

"You don't call Fawn. You don't call the police."

"Bianca!"

"No, listen—you don't know for sure if that was the missing painting or a fake. You're not an art expert. So

101

you can tell them your other call was a big mix-up, but you have some leads to follow and will report soon. Hey, for all we know, the painting in Sarah's trunk could have been a fake, right? I mean, haven't you seen *The Thomas Crowne Affair,* the movie where he paints fakes over real paintings and René Russo—"

"Yeah, yeah. I saw it." Her voice returned to a more normal tone.

"Before you do anything, look at the security tapes from tonight," I said, and immediately regretted it. What if the security tapes showed Hector carrying a suspicious package and heading for the dumpster door?

From our doorway, an expanding shaft of light appeared. Mom again.

"You girls still out here?" Translation: I can't enjoy watching television worrying about you two.

"We're coming in now, Mom," I said, looking directly at Connie. Translation: do we have a deal or not?

"Yeah, we'll be right there," Connie said. As we walked toward the steps, she whispered, "Okay. I want to talk to Kurt about this anyway."

The next morning, I awoke with an ache. Not a headache or a backache or a neck ache. It was an unfulfilled-desire ache, the kind of dry, choking feeling you get when you've kept yourself from doing something you really wanted to do.

I'd really, really wanted to talk to Doug the night before. I'd wanted to spend, oh, maybe a half hour or more on the phone with him (we have a "half hour" rule in our house, but sometimes Mom's not paying attention and I go over). And I wanted us to laugh and blab away the way we used to—about school, about our plans, about the Mistletoe Dance, and maybe even about the painting mess with Sarah.

But every time I'd thought of calling him, a switch would go on in my brain immediately cutting off the warm, fuzzy feelings I was having about him and replacing them with dark brooding. Brooding on why he had acted so attentive around Kerrie when I was supposed to be his girl. Brooding on why he'd picked her up first and dropped her off last on Saturday. Brooding about how he'd nearly ruined my Applebee's dining experience. And brooding as I thought of how I really couldn't share too much of the Sarah stuff with him or I might get her in trouble.

It was a cycle of despair, let me tell you. First, I'd start resenting him for abandoning me for Kerrie. Then I'd start resenting him for being jealous of Neville when I remained completely true blue to him. Then I'd start thinking that maybe he's jealous of me and Neville because he's feeling guilty about him and Kerrie.

Yes, that's where that brooding road led to—fantasies of unfaithful friends.

To make matters worse, Connie had been on the Internet a lot Sunday evening, looking up some stuff and then talking with Kurt on the phone—she has some cheapo-schmeapo cell plan she's locked into for a year, so she watches her minutes on that and hogs our phone instead. When I checked messages later, there was no Dougie-gram, which made me even more glum.

So, when I came down for breakfast Monday morning, I was in a crappy mood. Connie and Mom had already left—Mom for her office and Connie to hers. That left Tony and me, and Tony is at his all-time worst when there are no witnesses around.

"C'mon, I have to leave early," he said, looking at me in my pink terry-cloth robe and curling his upper lip to indicate I looked particularly unattractive that day.

"Why didn't you tell me that last night?" I said, grabbing the Frosted Flakes.

"I did, swamp thing." He put his bowl in the dishwasher.

"Did not."

"Did too."

"Did not."

We go in for sophisticated debate in the Balducci household.

After a few minutes of this back and forth, Tony told me I better be ready in five minutes or I was walking to school, then he vamoosed upstairs to brush his teeth. I snarled after him, but I don't think he heard. When I finished my breakfast and cleared the table, I was about to put the milk away when those darn poetry magnets caught my eye again.

Right before going to bed the night before, I'd rearranged them to read:

> *Funky survivor*
> *Cute groove*
> *Stars wild*
> *Kiss date*

I thought it was pretty cool—all those short little sentences.

Now, someone had rearranged them to read:

> *Groove funky*
> *Go wild*
> *Kiss stars*
> *Date freak*

"Date freak"? What the hey did that mean? Tony had to be doing this. Nasty, mean-spirited Tony. I ran upstairs and almost collided with him in the hallway.

"What has Doug ever done to you, huh? He's not a freak!" And I slammed the door on him as I ran into my bedroom to change.

"I have no idea what you're talking about, mutant woman," he shouted as he walked downstairs. I took that as an admission of guilt.

At school, my mood did not improve. In fact, everyone's mood seemed to be on the underside of happy. Doug barely said hello, instead giving me a quick, sulky smile that meant he was still steamed at my going off with Neville on Sunday. Kerrie was irritated because her locker lock was stuck for the umpteenth time this semester and she kept forgetting to get it replaced. And Sarah was in a funk because of Hector.

"I talked to Hector last night," Sarah said. "And he was nowhere near that part of the museum when it happened. He said the security tapes would prove it."

"You called him?" I asked. Was she tipping him off? Sheesh, Sarah!

"Well, he called me first. Remember?" she asked sheepishly.

Just then, the first bell rang and I could have screamed. I was choking on inner screams. I was beginning to feel like a model for that painting, "The Scream." Sarah, a nut about being on time, ran off to her first class while Kerrie pleaded for help with her locker. As I twirled and pulled and repositioned the thing, the locker hall emptied out and Kerrie spoke to me.

"I keep thinking about what you told me last night," Kerrie whispered. "About Neville and you."

"What about Neville and me?" I asked. Finally, the

lock came free. Good thing. I was going to be late for algebra.

"You know—what you told me. How you kissed." Kerrie pulled books from her locker and arranged others on a stack. Her locker was arranged as neatly as a display for the locker company while mine was always a jumble. "How did it make you feel?"

The whole episode with Neville now seemed light years in the past, and as I looked back, I couldn't quite figure out who that girl was who had let Neville kiss her, and why she had felt the crazy need to confess it to her best friend.

"I don't know. It was strange." I looked at the clock. I really had to get going. Kerrie slammed her locker shut and we walked out of the hall together. "I mean, I've never kissed a Brit before."

I was about to add that Brit or not, kissing Neville had been a huge mistake since my boyfriend was Doug. I was going to make a joke about how, if she told another living soul about it, I'd have to kill her, when we rounded the hallway corner and ran into the only living soul from whom I wanted to keep this juicy piece of information—Doug.

That day, I had algebra, history, English, and music. And every time the teacher asked a question, the first answer that popped into my head was: "Doug, it's not what you think."

Boys might be Silent Sams, but they're also pretty transparent. After he'd overheard the news that I'd kissed Neville, the look on Doug's face couldn't have been clearer. If I had been using poetry magnets to describe it, the verse would have gone something like this: "Boyfriend betrayed by silly steady/Crushed heart, bleeding hopes."

To make matters worse, we didn't see each other

much that day. I hoped to run into him at lunch, but he was nowhere to be seen. To make matters even worse than that, Kerrie was the one who knew why he wasn't there. He had a doctor's appointment, she announced over lunch.

"His physical. So he can play varsity tennis," she said, digging into a taco salad while I stared at my whole wheat and mozzarella. How did Kerrie know his intimate, personal schedule when I didn't?

Sarah came to the table, her tray holding a milk and her bagged lunch. When she sat down next to Kerrie, I should have been happy. They were speaking to each other again. Instead, I just moped.

Sarah was moping, too. As soon as she sat down, she started talking about Hector.

"The art gallery is looking into his past," she said while opening her milk. "They think he might be involved in this art theft thing."

Ouch. That meant Connie was looking into Hector's past. Maybe that's what she'd been doing on the Internet the night before. What else wasn't she telling me?

"What art theft thing?" Kerrie asked, after which I told her what I knew.

"Hector's a guard, right?" Kerrie asked.

"He's also an art student," Sarah volunteered, and she and I exchanged looks which, when translated, meant: okay, let's not tell Kerrie about the painting incident last night.

Sarah sipped some milk through a straw. "That's why they're looking at him. And because he was around. When it happened. When the works disappeared."

"Are the police questioning him?" Kerrie asked.

Sarah shook her head "no." "The museum is keeping it quiet."

"How come?" Kerrie asked. "Don't they have a responsibility to turn this information over to the police?"

Sarah's color faded, and she was pale to begin with. The way Kerrie had said "turn this information over to the police" sent chills down my spine, too. It was as if she was really saying "turn Hector over to the police."

"Just because Hector's an art student doesn't mean he's a forger," I jumped in. "Why zero in on him?" Funny I should be sticking up for Hector. I kind of suspected him, too.

Sarah didn't say anything, but Kerrie did. "Does Hector have a record?"

Sarah slowly nodded. "But it was a long time ago. Two years. He was picked up with some boys who'd stolen a car. He was let go."

"How'd he get his job with a record?" Kerrie asked. "I mean, I thought you couldn't get hired for a security job if you'd had a run-in with the law."

Sarah looked down.

"He didn't tell them!" I surmised. Sarah nodded her head.

"You mean he lied," Kerrie said in a "he's getting what he deserves" kind of voice.

Sarah's head shot up. "He wasn't sure it mattered. He was just a high school kid at the time."

Kerrie shrugged as if to say it did matter. Her indifference sent pink into Sarah's cheeks. "He's trying to make a living to put himself through college. His mother is on disability. He doesn't even know his dad." Her voice quivered and her eyes grew watery. Sarah had had her own "run-in" with the law recently. She'd been connected with an identity theft ring until Kerrie's dad helped bail her out of trouble. So it was only natural that she was sympathetic to others in trouble, particularly if one of the "others" happened to be a fellow she liked.

While Sarah's background certainly illustrated that one should not automatically be considered a criminal because of a shady past, I wondered about Hector. I mean, who's to say he wasn't up to something, especially if he did have cash worries? He might be looking for a way to make a quick buck. And if he, as a security guard, had access to art works worth thousands of dollars, temptation might overrule good judgment. As Connie would have said, he had motive and opportunity. And if he was an art student, he had know-how, too. I felt sick for Sarah.

But I kept those thoughts to myself, which is a good thing, because Kerrie voiced them for me.

"I know you like Hector," she said to Sarah in a voice supposed to sound sympathetic but instead sounded condescending, "but if he does have money problems, selling some valuable paintings on the black market would certainly be a way of fixing them." She reached over and patted Sarah's hand, but Sarah immediately withdrew it and turned an even deeper shade of red.

"Hector is not an art thief!" she exploded, loud enough for some kids at a nearby table to turn our way. She lowered her voice. "He's being unfairly targeted. Why don't they look at all the other guards? Why just him?"

Kerrie smiled. Well, actually, it was more like a smirk. "Maybe because he's a part-time art student, too?"

Sarah opened her mouth to reply but didn't have time to respond. Our student government president, no-nonsense Bethany Christopher, was at the cafeteria mike making some announcements about food drives and drama club meetings and the Mistletoe Dance. I zeroed in on that last nugget of info.

"Tickets for the Mistletoe Dance are now on sale in the school office before and after school. Because we're holding the dance in the cafeteria this year, fire regulations say we can only accommodate 1,100 people, so get your tickets fast or you'll be left in the cold."

Kerrie groaned. "The cafeteria? I thought they'd gotten Martin's West for the dance. That's where they have it every year."

"Somebody screwed up the reservation," Sarah said. "And when they realized it, all the dates were booked."

At that moment, I didn't really care where the dance was being held. My stomach started flip-flopping into knots as a new problem presented itself. Would Doug buy dance tickets in time?

It's not that Doug is a procrastinator. No, he's just a normal guy. And any other time, he would probably zip on down to the office to snag the tickets so we wouldn't be "left out in the cold." But after this morning, when Doug had overheard me talking about kissing Neville, would he still want to go with me to the dance? Would he still want to be my boyfriend?

No longer hungry, I wrapped up the rest of my sandwich and threw it back in the paper bag. Kerrie started talking about the dress she was going to wear to the Mistletoe Dance—the black velvet number she'd tried on at The Limited—and how she was going even if she didn't have a date.

But I was lost in my own thoughts, staring into space and wondering how I'd managed to lose my boyfriend in such record time. Sarah seemed to be lost in her thoughts as well, probably of Hector and his problems with the museum.

Eventually, Kerrie noticed neither of us was paying attention to her chatter and threw in a line designed to grab our thoughts.

"I thought I'd dye my hair orange to go with the dress," she said nonchalantly.

"Sounds nice," Sarah said.

"Huh?" I said.

Kerrie laughed. "You both were in la-la land," she said. "Bianc, why don't you call me tonight and we'll talk about your Doug problem."

"What Doug problem?" Sarah asked.

Kerrie turned to her. "Oh, nothing."

I let out a quick sigh. Or maybe it was more of a snort. Rule Number One of Friendships: don't hint at secrets in front of other friends. Sarah might as well know.

"Neville kissed me, and Doug found out," I said.

"What!?" Sarah looked at me as if I had three heads. "And how'd Doug find out?"

I was about to tell her he'd heard it from the horse's mouth, then neigh like a pony, but the bell rang, ending lunch period. "I'll explain it later," I said to her, and left.

My afternoon was as gloomy as my morning, maybe even gloomier. I managed to foul up an algebra test pretty badly by failing to check my work, and I knew Mom would not like that since she's always telling me to check my work so my smarts don't get ahead of my brain. And Doug was nowhere to be seen because he *obviously* was out of school early for his physical, and I hadn't even had a chance to ask Kerrie how she knew that, and I didn't know what I would say to Doug if I saw him anyway.

I had to go home alone that day. Kerrie was staying after school to work on the literary magazine, and Sarah was going to her internship. As I stood at the bus stop shivering in my lightweight blazer, I saw a familiar car wending its way through traffic in front of the school—Connie's. Connie was coming to pick me up! What parallel universe was I living in?

"Glad I caught you," she said after I got in. "I was coming by this way and thought I'd see if you needed a ride."

Who is this woman and what has she done with my real sister?

Connie never gives me rides if she can help it. She could have an appointment scheduled with my principal at the end of the school day and she'd still let me ride the bus home, making up some excuse about why she couldn't commit to bringing me home.

As she maneuvered through traffic, she asked me what I was getting Mom for Christmas. We talked about pooling our money so we could get her a nicer gift, maybe a day at a spa or something. Then Connie finally got around to the real reason she was being nice to me.

"So, did you think any more about what I said?" she asked.

"What? What did you say?"

"About putting a word in for me—with Witherspoon's son."

Mental groan. The last thing I needed to do now was talk with Neville Witherspoon. When I didn't say anything, she continued.

"He called, you know."

"What?" I asked.

"I checked the voice mail at home, from my office. And Neville called you. I saved the message."

"Connie!"

"Hey, what's so bad about that? He sounds like a nice enough guy."

"I have a boyfriend, in case you hadn't noticed." Right. More like *had* a boyfriend, if you know what I mean. "Besides, isn't Mr. Witherspoon on the museum board? You're working for the board. You can get to him that way."

"I work for the staff, not the board," she said, "though, after I finish this job, I can use it to get in to see him. But it wouldn't hurt for you to help me out now with Neville. He's a bird in the hand."

When I didn't say anything, she continued.

"I'm not asking you to marry the guy. You only need to ask him how I can get in to see his dad. That's all, for crying out loud." She honked at a car that wasn't moving fast enough when the light turned green. After a couple blocks of silent driving, she spoke again.

"All right. I'll make a deal with you. You talk to Neville Witherspoon about me, and I'll help you with something. Name your price. What do you want most?"

What I wanted most was to get back in Doug's good graces, but I doubted Connie could deliver on that. Hmmm . . . but maybe she could help me out in that regard all the same.

"Another phone line. I want another phone line so I can stay on the Internet as long as I like."

Connie shot me a glance, her mouth twisted up to one side as if she admired my negotiating skill. "I'll see what I can do."

"What do you think will happen to Hector?" I asked after we drove for a few more minutes.

"Don't know." Oh, she knew all right. She just wasn't saying. Bummer for him and for poor Sarah.

As for me, hey—things could be worse. My boyfriend might be mad at me, but at least he wasn't an art thief.

"What did you find out from the security tapes?" I

asked, remembering Connie had said she was going to look at them.

"Nothing. Big goose egg. They're as clean as a whistle."

"What do you mean?"

"They don't show anything. Nobody in that part of the museum—nobody in the hallway leading to the door out to the dumpster. So the thief probably used a different exit."

We drove for a few seconds, then a thought came to me so fast and hard I almost fell over.

"Connie!" I said, turning toward her. "The tapes had to show *someone* in that hallway—Sarah was there, remember?"

Connie's mouth fell open and I knew exactly what she was thinking: "Darn it, Bianca! You just came up with something I should've thought of."

But there was no time for thinking. She pointed up ahead.

"Hey—that's Hector!"

I leaned forward and peered through the window.

"How can you tell? It's the back of a head."

"He turned around a minute ago, looked at something in the backseat." A light turned green and we inched forward.

"Let's follow him!" I shouted in true detective fashion.

Chapter Fourteen

"It's too hard to follow someone when you only have one car," Connie lectured me. "Usually when you're following someone, you need a partner, maybe two. It's complicated." Just then Hector turned left onto a street leading into the city.

"Come on, we can do it! Just for a little while."

Connie didn't say anything, but she turned where Hector had turned.

"Up there!" I said, pointing. "Maybe he's going to turn there. Be prepared to get in the right lane. No, wait, he's staying in the left one. Hold on, I think I see his turn signal—"

"Shut up, Bianca. I can't concentrate!"

"What's there to concentrate on? Your foot on the gas pedal, your hands on the steering wheel . . ."

Connie didn't appreciate my helpful driving suggestions and gave out a disgusted snort as she maneuvered her car through heavy city traffic. Two cars ahead, I could see Hector's cruddy black Impala lumbering along Mount Royal Avenue.

"Damn. I hate Bolton Hill. Always get lost here," Connie muttered under her breath. She turned right on a street just as Hector shifted to the left lane and went straight.

"Hey!" I pointed out the front window. "He went thataway!"

"I know, I know." Connie slowed down, glanced over her shoulder, and pulled off a quick U-turn on the small side street. "I thought he was going to turn."

Bolton Hill is a funny neighborhood. Like ours, it's a mixture of renovated homes side by side with houses that look like their owners stopped trying. As we cruised by some of the better places, I helpfully pointed out decorating items I liked. "Look at that flower box! Did you see that window treatment?" I'm sure Connie really appreciated this. She showed it by letting out a little groan of delight.

"This is why you need more than one person to follow a car," she said, speeding up to see if she could locate Hector again. "One to follow right behind, another to stay several car lengths behind that. This one-car stuff sucks!"

"Guess I'll have to get my driver's license," I said, imagining our future partnership.

She shot me a quick look. "Guess you'll have to get a car, too."

"There he is!" I pointed to a block ahead. Hector's car was double-parked outside a seedy-looking corner building with boards across its lower floor windows.

Connie crawled past while I scooted down in my seat so Hector wouldn't see me.

"Get up. He's not there." Connie pulled the car around to the next side street and parked it two inches into legal. When I peeked up and over, I saw what she meant. Hector's car sat there, but Hector was nowhere to be seen.

"Wonder what's in there," I said, pointing to the ratty-looking building and imagining an art forgery clubhouse kind of thing.

Just then, Hector came back out and I slipped down in the seat again. Connie exhaled sharply while she peered in her rearview mirror.

"What's he doing?" I whispered.

"Getting into his car." She spoke without moving her lips, so it was hard to understand her.

"Now what?"

"He's looking at something."

"At what?"

"Something he brought out of that house with him." She glanced at me. "Shh . . . he might hear you."

"He's not going to hear me! We're a half block away and I'm on the car floor. When was the last time you cleaned this car, anyway?" I pulled an old drugstore receipt from the bottom of my shoe. "Besides, he could recognize you as well as me. After all, you met him at the museum, too, and . . ."

"He's looking at something. Something rolled up. Except now's he unrolled it."

"Like a painting, you mean?" My heart started thumping so loudly I was sure Hector could hear it no matter how many blocks were between us. Hector was guilty! Maybe Connie was right—if you hear hoofbeats, think first of horses, not zebras. Hector had artistic talent, motive, opportunity . . .

"Yeah, like a painting. He's studying it."

"Can you see what it is?"

"Nope. Only the underside of the paper. It's cream-colored paper. Something old looking." She leaned over to my side of the car, our faces inches apart. I made a mental note to ask Connie where she'd gotten her earrings—little points of cobalt blue. Pretty classy.

"What are you doing?" I asked.

"Looking busy. He's leaving. Don't want him to recognize me."

I could hear a car passing by just beyond the curb. Once its noise was safely in the distance, I got up. Hector's car was gone.

"Come on," I said, opening my car door. "Let's see what's in this building."

"Bianca!" Connie quickly followed, slamming her door shut behind her. "This isn't safe. Let me take you home."

"And let you come back and do this on your own? No way!" I strode off to the building with Connie quickly in pursuit.

It was a heavy, dark brownstone—a curved tower at the corner and cracked windows on upper floors. Hector must have entered by a side door because the front door was covered with boards, as were the lower floor windows. We skulked around to the side, to an out-of-place modern door that seemed to have been plucked from a suburban colonial and attached to this old house as an afterthought.

Connie nudged me out of the way. "Let me. You shouldn't be doing this. I'm a professional." Professional or not, Connie didn't do anything exotic. She just crept up to the door, stood on tiptoes, and peered through narrow windows set at the top of the door.

Just as she looked in, we both heard three sharp *kerthwangs!* in quick succession.

I gulped. A gun? Did someone have a gun in there? Were we coming upon some kind of art forgery gangland killing scene?

Connie's eyes widened.

"What is it?" I asked. "Let me see." I pulled at her

jacket just as I'd done when we were little kids and she was racing ahead of me. Some things never change, you know. "Is it a gun? Is somebody dead in there?"

"Nope." She relaxed and moved away from the door. "Except maybe a doornail. That was a nail gun. Someone's renovating this place."

Okay, I admit it. I was disappointed. I thought we'd stumbled onto something here, something that would have earned us some accolades from the local police chief, some cheesy photo shaking hands with him or her while a headline blared: "Amateur Sleuth Uncovers Kajillion Dollar Art Thieves."

My disappointment immediately morphed into relief, however. Lack of violence is a good thing. But renovation?

Before I could think this through, Connie was tugging on the door handle and opening it. What the—?

"Excuse me," she said sweetly to the three burly guys in the dusty room in front of us. They stopped what they were doing and looked at her like she was an escapee from a mental institution. We Balduccis have that effect on people.

"Excuse me, but I was wondering if you could help me. I'm an art student at the Maryland Institute and I thought I just saw someone carrying the most exquisite painting . . ." She even spoke with a southern drawl. I looked at her like she was nuts. Again, a Balducci trait.

The oldest looking of the crew stepped forward and wiped sweat off his brow. "You mean what Hector was carrying?"

"I don't know his name. Some dark fellow. Just came out of here."

"That wasn't a painting. It was a sketch of this." He pointed upward to the ceiling. Above us was a mural of chubby cherubs and fluffy clouds. It was heavily damaged—by water and peeling plaster. "Hector's repairing it for us. You want his number?" One of the other men chuckled.

"No, no thanks. My, what a lovely image. Mid-nineteenth century, I'd say. Neo-romantic with touches of post-modern Gothic."

"Constance," I said sweetly in a not-so-hot drawl that sounded more like a vampire in Sunday school, "we shan't stay long, shall we? We must be going. Mummy will be so worried." Oh yes, and I threw in some Brit, too. I'm sure it impressed them.

Connie and I left, rushing back to the car before they called the Bad Accent Police on us.

"So he's not a thief," I said triumphantly while Connie started the car. "He's just doing some part-time work. Neat, too. Looks like fun." I began to wonder if I should include art restorer on my list of possible careers. Naw, scratch that. I forgot about the main prerequisite—artistic talent.

Connie badly wanted that Witherspoon account. Not only did she speak up for a new phone line at dinner, but she offered to do the dishes when it was my night. Her new helpfulness was almost enough to cheer me through my doldrums. *Almost.* Now that the day was ending, I couldn't quite shake the feeling that I had done something really bad to Doug.

I tried to call him as soon as I got home, but he wasn't in and I didn't want to leave a message for fear he wouldn't call me back. No point in painting a HURT ME target on myself, right?

I figured I'd do some homework, then reach for the phone and try him around 7:30.

At 7:23, however, Connie popped into my room, her

cell phone in hand. I know it was exactly 7:23 because, ever since I came up with the call-Doug plan, I'd been counting down the minutes to my self-imposed zero hour. I was lying across my bed, studying for History.

Okay, okay, I was pretending to study.

"Why don't you call Neville back?" Connie said, holding the cell phone out to me. This was serious if she was offering the cell.

"I'm supposed to call Doug at 7:30," I told her. I smiled sweetly. "But I'll try Neville after that."

She didn't miss a beat. "You can call Neville first. Tony's on the phone right now, anyway."

Ah-ha, that was the real reason for the cell. Call me crazy, but I doubted if Connie would lend me the use of her cell phone to call Doug. My guess was that the cell offer was for Neville phone calls only.

With a sigh of resignation, I sat up and held out my hand. After she plopped the tiny phone in my palm, she pulled out a piece of paper with her other hand.

"Here's his number," she said. "I wrote it down for you."

I narrowed my eyes and took the paper, trying to telegraph in the broadest possible terms that this was not something I enjoyed doing. I wanted her to be an expert witness in my good-girlfriend trial, you see. ("So, Miss Constance Balducci, did your sister *like* calling Neville Witherspoon?" That was the key question I imagined the prosecutor, who looked a lot like Doug, asking. And Connie would answer, "No, sir. She was extremely reluctant to make the call. I had to force her to do it.")

"Do you mind?" I asked after punching in the numbers. Connie just shrugged and walked out of the room. As the call rang through, I got up and closed the door.

"Witherspoon residence," a maid-like voice answered.

"Is Neville there, please?"

A few seconds later, Neville was on the phone, cheerily thanking me for getting back to him.

"The reason I was calling, love, is I have an extra ticket to a gala of some sort. Tomorrow night. Some charity event at the symphony, I think. Would you be so kind as to escort me?"

With no regret, I explained that I couldn't accompany him. No dates allowed on school nights. That was the Law of the (Balducci) Land. Thank you, Mom.

Then I had a veritable brainstorm. Connie! Connie could accompany him! Sure, she was nearly ten years his senior, but she was pretty cool looking, and she was the one who wanted to get close to the Witherspoon clan, not me.

"Hey, but my sister could go," I said, and launched into a description of what a babe she was and how interesting she was and how much she would like to meet him—how she'd told me so after I'd described him to her. Yes, I was pouring it on, and not feeling a twinge of guilt for doing so.

To my surprise—and maybe even a little disappointment—Neville didn't bat an eyelash at this sister-swap. If anything, he jumped on the idea with tremendous enthusiasm.

"That sounds marvelous. I can pick her up at 7:00. Or would she prefer I meet her at the Meyerhoff Hall?"

Knowing Connie liked an exit strategy for new dates, I had mercy on her and suggested she meet him at the hall, and arranged for the rendezvous.

My heart lighter, I chatted easily with Neville for a few minutes and got off the phone feeling like a heavy weight had been lifted off my shoulders. I'd killed two birds with one stone—I'd been nice to Connie and I'd gotten rid of Neville! Woohoo!

All silver linings have clouds, though. In the hallway a second later, I nearly collided with Tony, which meant he was off the phone. While this brightened my mood considerably, our conversation did not.

"Doug called," he said as he headed for the bathroom. "Connie said you were on the phone with that Neville guy, so I told Doug you'd call him back." He shut the door behind him.

What? "On the phone with that Neville guy"? Did Tony tell Doug that?

"Tony!" I shouted through the door. "What did you tell Doug?"

"Huh? I don't remember. You were on the phone."

I knew I wouldn't get anything out of him, so I sagged back to Connie's room. Her door opened as I approached.

"What did Tony tell Doug when he called?" I asked.

"I don't know. What did Neville say?" She held out her hand for her phone, which I started to give her, then retracted at the last minute.

"Wait a second. Bargain. I'll tell you about Neville— and it's good, by the way—if you tell me precisely what Tony told Doug when you told Tony I was on the phone with Neville."

"Look, I don't remember, okay? I didn't think it was something I'd be interrogated on. C'mon, tell me about Witherspoon. Can I see his dad or not?"

I knew I could hold out and make her life miserable for the evening, but what was the point? Chances are she was telling the truth—that she truly didn't take note of what Tony had told Doug. Some private investigator she was! So I went ahead and returned her phone while I told her about her terrific date with Neville. She moaned and groaned about the usual things—the age difference, the fact that Neville wasn't her type (which gave me plenty of opportunity to rib her about the guy who currently was "her type"—namely, Kurt, "the Hunky Man"), and the fact she had nothing to wear. But all in all, I think she was pleased to have the opportunity to talk with Neville, who, she was sure, would get her in to his father's office.

I, meanwhile, was not pleased. I tried calling Doug back, prepared to tell him the full truth about the phone call and even throw in a line about how "forward" Neville had been, which would then lead me to toss off a line about how he even "kissed me good night the other night, which I thought was so rude."

But Doug's line was in use—the voice mail picked up immediately. I tried a few more times in the next half hour—to no avail. So I decided to call Kerrie to pour out my troubles. No dice there, either. Her line was tied up as well.

I sat down at the computer and, firing up the Internet and e-mail, IMed Kerrie, letting her know I just tried to call her.

She wrote back immediately: "i'm on the phone with doug."

Chapter Fourteen

"On the phone with Doug."

The words were like a knife to my heart. After Kerrie IMed me she was on the phone with my boyfriend, I made polite cyberchat for a few minutes, then wrote a cheery, "i need to talk to doug myself, so i'm gonna go now," which any half-intelligent person knew really meant "get off the phone so I can talk to my boyfriend!"

But when I tried his number again, the voice mail still picked up almost instantaneously, which meant Kerrie had either ignored my hint or didn't get it. I can't imagine she didn't get it.

In fact, she didn't get it for hours. I tried his number five more times before going to bed, and each time the line was in use. I tossed and turned all night.

I was in a foul mood the next day, and my mood perfectly matched the weather. It was raining—a soaking, heavy downpour that left none of us unscathed. Even those with umbrellas were wet, and I'd forgotten mine, so I was drenched. My sophisticated new haircut lay matted against my head, and I was sure I looked like a wet dog after a reluctant bath, except maybe not as cute.

Rule of the Universe: At the very moment when you're

looking your most uncute, expect your boyfriend to want a heart-to-heart talk with you.

Actually, I was the one who decided on the heart-to-heart. I'm not good at waiting for bad news. No, far better to meet it head on than loll around in it, right? So when Doug came into the locker hall that Tuesday, I was loaded for bear. I marched right over to him and said, in a charmingly accusatory way, "I tried to reach you all night last night, but you were on the phone with Kerrie."

He stared at me for a second like I was nuts. Then he grimaced, threw his books in his locker, and leaned against it.

"I was only on with her for a few minutes. My brother was using the phone."

Oh well. So much for my grand confrontation. Somehow, I felt disappointed. Okay, time to switch to a new tack.

"Did you get the Mistletoe Dance tickets?" I asked, again in that attractive voice that combines whining with a dash of irritation.

"No." Then, the coup de grâce—the words that would haunt me all day. "I didn't know if you still wanted to go with me," Doug said.

The bell rang. The bell always rings at the wrong time. But we still had a few minutes' grace period. Unfortunately, I didn't get to use them to reconcile our rift because Sarah breezed in late and her locker was near Doug's. When she saw us together, she looked at me with mopey eyes and told me she needed to talk with me.

"About Hector," she said. "I talked to him last night. He's thinking of quitting."

Sarah and Kerrie must have come in together because Kerrie soon joined our little gathering. At the mention of Hector, Kerrie scowled. Sarah noticed.

"It's serious, Ker. He could be in real trouble," Sarah said.

"Right. 'Real' being the key word there," Kerrie said.

"What's that supposed to mean?" Sarah asked. After shoving her lunch inside the locker, she twirled her combination lock and quickly grabbed her books for the day.

"Hector has a record. He's a likely suspect. It doesn't take a rocket scientist . . ." Kerrie said, shrugging her shoulders.

The blood rushed to Sarah's face, turning it beet red.

"Hector's not like that! He's a good person. He was just in the wrong place at the wrong time!" She looked at me as if I was supposed to help out here, but I had reached my trouble-quota already today.

Doug, however, decided to once again play mediator, and, as usual, stepped in on Kerrie's side!

"I think Kerrie's just trying to look out for you," he said to Sarah. "She doesn't want you to get hurt."

Now it was my turn to steam and stew. So that's what Doug and Kerrie were IM'ing each other about last night—Sarah and Hector? Once again, my friend Kerrie was using Doug as a sympathy sponge. It wasn't fair and I was tired of it.

I looked at Sarah. "I'll talk to Connie," I told her, and I knew she'd know what I was saying—I'd try to find out more info and pass it along.

Kerrie let out a little snort. The second bell rang, and with the morning grace period over, we had to hightail it to class or be marked late.

"What?" I asked Kerrie.

"Nothing," she said in a harrumphy kind of voice. "Connie might find out something Sarah doesn't want to face."

Sarah slammed her locker shut. "You just don't like Hector because he's a Latino."

Kerrie practically sputtered with indignation. "I can't believe you said that! You're accusing me of being a . . . a . . . racist!"

"If the shoe fits . . ." Sarah said.

Oh man, this was bad. Really bad. Kerrie was accusing Sarah's boyfriend of being a criminal. Sarah was accusing Kerrie of being a racist. Doug wasn't getting the Mistletoe Dance tickets. Where would it all end?

"Look, let's . . . calm down," I was about to say. But Doug did me one better. He walked over to Kerrie, who looked like she was going to cry, and put his arm around her shoulder. Now *I* felt like crying!

"We can talk later," Doug said to no one in particular. And we all went off to our homerooms.

But we didn't talk later. We just brooded in our separate little stew pots. I became so depressed about the whole thing that I didn't seek out Doug to continue our conversation because I became terribly afraid of where it might lead. Although I'd not done anything wrong with Neville (okay, the kiss was a mistake, but I wasn't planning on repeating it), I was beginning to suspect that Doug was getting ready to dump me and take up with Kerrie. If that happened, I'd lose both my boyfriend and my girlfriend, and my heart would be broken.

It was only natural, then, that I gravitated toward Sarah. At lunch, during which Kerrie sat with some other girls, Sarah talked more about Hector and the museum. To keep myself from going bonkers over my Doug and Kerrie problems, I paid sharp attention.

"Does Hector have any idea who it might be?" I asked Sarah.

She scowled a little, as if she didn't like fingering people, even if doing so meant clearing Hector. "Well, he's not too crazy about Ms. Dexter."

"Why would she be doing something like this?"

"Publicity? I don't know. He said something about how it could draw attention to the museum. You remember that big fuss over the Brooklyn Museum?"

Yeah, I remembered. We had discussed it in religion class one day. The Brooklyn Museum had launched an exhibit of new works that included some stuff considered sacrilegious by some Catholics. No matter which side you were on in that debate, one thing was clear— the museum got tons of attention. Not bad for a place that had always played second fiddle to places like the Metropolitan Museum of Art and the Museum of Modern Art.

"Well, if she wanted that kind of publicity," I said, "she would have gone to the police and made a big deal over it."

"If she's the criminal, she wouldn't want the police involved," Sarah said.

"Then how does she get the publicity without the police involved?"

"I don't know." Sarah said it so sadly I figured this was a point neither she nor Hector had figured out yet.

Before I left school that day, I passed the office, where girls and boys stood waiting to purchase Mistletoe Dance tickets. I didn't see Doug in the line. In fact, I saw him rushing past the office door to the walkway outside. For all I knew, Kerrie was out there waiting for him.

It turns out, though, that Kerrie was staying after school for drama club, so Sarah offered to take me home.

Once there, I saw a note on the kitchen table from Connie.

"Mom says fix spaghetti."

I did my homework and got dinner started. While working in the kitchen, I rearranged the poetry magnets yet again, this time to read: "All over/boyfriend gone/life sucks." I wasn't in the mood for florid phrases.

At least one of the Balduccis was happy that evening, though. When Connie breezed in right before supper, she was perkier than a Christmas ornament.

"I got in!" she announced, shaking off her raincoat. "I've got an appointment to see Witherspoon! Just agreeing to go out with Neville must have done the trick!"

"Woohoo," I said in a rather subdued tone of voice.

As we ate dinner a little while later, Mom peppered us with questions about our lives. Tony answered with grunts, Connie with vague replies about how things were "moving along," and I just mumbled, "okay."

"We need to finish that green velvet dress," Mom said, pointing her fork at me. "We all get so busy this time of year. I'm afraid if we don't get on it now, we'll be rushing around at the last minute."

I didn't have the heart to tell her that maybe I wouldn't even need the dress, so I just nodded my head and acted like I had a mouthful of food and couldn't answer. But after dinner, she made good on her offer and had me try the thing on for a fitting.

Not that it mattered, since my Mistletoe Dance prospects were being sucked relentlessly down the drainpipe of lost dreams, but the dress wasn't shaping up. Don't get me wrong—I love my mom and know she means well. But her sewing skills are inconsistent. Sometimes she can make a really fine dress that looks like it came from a high-priced boutique. Other times, she can make skirts that look like they were whipped up by a de-

signer whose inspiration was Picasso during his cubist period. This green velvet was falling into the latter category.

While she pulled pins from her mouth to hold up the
hem, I stared at myself in the mirror, trying to determine
exactly what was wrong. Perhaps it was the way the
seams at the shoulders bunched awkwardly on one side
while laying flat on the other. Or maybe it was the way
the heavy fabric bubbled at the empire seam below the
bust, creating a sort of maternity dress effect. Or maybe
it was the color. It had seemed like a nice-looking jade
under the bright fluorescent lights of the fabric store. In
our house, though, it looked like mashed peas—kind of
dull and sickly.

Normally, this sort of thing would cause me to search
for tactful reasons I couldn't wear the thing, or at least
ways to secretly destroy it when Mom wasn't looking,
thus justifying the purchase of a real dress. But in my
mood, with my prospects of even going to the dance
now dimmed, I stood soldier-straight, reconciled to my
fate. If Mom enjoyed pinning the hem, let her pin the
hem. It was my gift to her, right?

After our seamstress session, I thanked her, ran upstairs to change, and then stopped in Connie's room for
a chat about the Hector situation. She was grabbing up
a bunch of beauty products and getting ready to take a
shower.

She was in such a good mood that she listened patiently.
Even so, she didn't have any good news to offer. Like
everyone else, she was assuming Hector might be involved.

"The Fawn Dexter theory doesn't work," she said, and
then gave me the very reason I'd given to Sarah at lunch—
if publicity was the motive, where was the publicity?

"But we know Hector didn't do it—he's not on the
tape," I said weakly.

"Nobody was on the tape, as you wisely pointed out, kiddo. The tapes were switched with one from an earlier time frame. I found out this afternoon."

"So it was someone who had access to the security tapes," I said. Like a security guard. *Gulp.*

"The best thing you can do for Sarah," she said ominously, "is tell her to stay away from the guy." With that, she went into the bathroom to get ready for her "date."

As a thank-you for my help with the case and the new Witherspoon account, Connie showed pity on me and actually shared some of the case information.

Well, maybe not actually shared. But hey, she did leave the file out on her bed when she knew I was home, so that's a form of sharing, right? She had to know I'd come in her room and look at it.

In the file, Connie had copies of reports and interviews, and background info that she herself had gathered. The bad news was that Hector had a couple of hefty debts to pay off—his student loans and some credit card bills. The good news was that Hector was a top student in college. He supported a younger sister and sent money to an aunt in Mexico every month.

But here was the thing that grabbed me—he had a great job lined up. According to Connie's notes, Hector had interviewed with a prestigious graphic design firm in New York City and was told that he was a "prime candidate" for a slot they had opening next year. They would even pay for night classes so he could finish his degree at a New York art college. A copy of the letter making this offer was in her file.

Now a guy with debts might do something stupid to make the money he needed to clear up his financial mess. But a guy with a future wouldn't risk it, especially a guy like Hector, who appeared to be on the road to responsibility. Call me crazy, but I just didn't see it.

Besides, Neville had said it would be hard to sell the stuff on the black market, and I couldn't envision Hector taking contemporary pieces from the museum and putting them into his own private collection. Connie had included a few photos of Hector's work—they were all realistic pieces. The few "abstracts" were graceful explosions of color that resembled photographs of the Northern Lights. He just didn't seem to have the taste for the stuff that was faked.

Speaking of which, one of the pieces that had been taken from the museum was called "Trapezoid with Stencil III." An oil on canvas from 1979, it was something that practically anybody could have done, even me. It was a canvas in the shape of a trapezoid, painted a pale blue (kind of the color of my bedroom), and in the middle of the thing was pasted a stencil of a rose—the kind you get at craft stores. It was described thus:

"Beckoning with a drenched shade of blue evocative of old wall finishes" (hey, was I right, or what?), " 'Trapezoid' captures the blandness of popular culture while gently parodying decorative arts with the burnished stencil."

Huh? "Blandness of popular culture"? I felt like showing this artist my poetry magnets. They weren't bland. They were downright jumpin'. I began to wonder how much "Trapezoid" was worth. And I thought again of Neville's theory—that maybe it wasn't an art thief at work but a frustrated artist sending some kind of message.

I was still musing on these questions when Connie rolled in after eleven. Grabbing my robe, I met her in the hallway.

"How was it?" I asked, yawning.

"Okay. Kind of juvenile." She smiled at me. "But I'll be on retainer with Witherspoon's firm by tomorrow." She walked into her room. "Hey! Someone's been in my file."

"You left it out!" I said in defense of my snooping. "Besides, I think I can help."

Connie unbuttoned her jacket and hung it up in the closet.

"I *really* need my own place," she said. But she didn't kick me out. Instead, she sat on the edge of the bed, pulled the file towards her, and looked up at me.

"Okay, shoot. What's your theory?"

It wasn't my theory, of course. It was Neville's. But that didn't stop me from spouting it out as if I were some art fraud expert. When I finished, she twisted her mouth to one side and narrowed her eyes. Tapping her fingers on the now-closed file, she said, "You know, that's not a bad thought. Neville mentioned that to me as well."

That darn Neville.

"And," she continued, "it certainly implicates Hector."

"But why? He has a job lined up, a good future . . ."

"Well, Miss Smartypants, if you looked through the file, you saw what kind of artist he is. He doesn't go in for this throw-the-paint-at-the-wall-and-see-where-it-sticks stuff . . ."

"Abstract expressionism," I interrupted. "I think that's what they call it."

"Whatever. He paints real pictures."

"Yeah. And he's going to get paid for them. You saw how he has a job lined up. Why would he jeopardize that with a juvenile prank?" Hmmph—I can use that word, too.

"Who knows?" Connie shrugged her shoulders and yawned. "I've seen smart people do dumber things."

"I just don't see it. He sends money to an aunt. He's got a job lined up. He's working his way through school. When people do dumb things, they usually have a pattern of doing dumb things."

"Are you speaking from experience?" she asked. When I curled my lip at her, she continued, "He has that record."

"That was long ago. He's reformed. Like Sarah."

Connie leaned back. Her leg twitched while she thought.

"I have to admit," she said at last, "that I don't have a gut feeling he's the one."

"There you go."

"But what I can't figure out is why somebody would pull this kind of prank in this way." She sat up straight. "I mean, if you're trying to make a point about this, this—"

"Abstract Expressionism," I offered.

"Whatever—if you're trying to tell the world that it's a bunch of hooey, shouldn't you be announcing it in a more spectacular way? Nobody but the board knows about the thefts."

"Maybe the criminal didn't plan it that way."

"What do you mean?"

"Maybe they expected it to leak out."

Connie yawned. "Look, I'm beat and you have school tomorrow."

That was my cue to leave, but as I went, I thought of ways to help solve the case. In the morning, I'd talk to Sarah about a new hunch I had.

Chapter Sixteen

In the morning, however, both Connie and I had our answer to the question on what the fraud artist would do to gain public attention.

On the front page of the *Baltimore Sun*, in the lower right corner, was a story about the whole affair, with Connie mentioned as the private investigator the museum hired!

Connie was furious. As I sat at breakfast, she was answering a phone call from Fawn Dexter, and I could tell from her red face and numerous "yes, Fawn," "no, Fawn" responses that whatever Fawn was saying was not of the "have a nice day" variety. When she got off the phone, she let out a frustrated growl.

"You didn't tell any of your friends about the investigation, did you?" she snapped at me. She grabbed a bowl from the kitchen cabinet and plopped down at the table across from me.

"No!" Which was the truth. I had no friends—only bickering, squabbling acquaintances.

"Well, *somebody* leaked *something* to the press," Connie hissed.

"It wasn't me! Why do you always think it's me when something goes wrong?"

Just then, Mom walked in the room. "What are you girls arguing about this morning?" she asked as she got herself a cup of coffee and snapped on her wristwatch. Tony had a really early class so Mom was driving me to school that day.

"Connie thinks I blabbed to the Sunpapers about her investigation of the museum case." I jabbed my finger at the newspaper, and my mother joined us at the table.

As she read, she nodded her head. "Yes, I'd heard about this. I really thought it was a mistake for the museum to keep it under wraps. It undermines public trust in a public institution," she said, sipping her coffee.

Connie and I looked at each other with wide eyes. Mom knew about it? Was she the leak? Before I had a chance to ask any questions, Connie jumped in with her own.

"How did you . . ."

"Baltimore is really a very small town," Mom said. "And it gets even smaller when you're dealing with the arts crowd."

Hmmm . . . Mom worked for the District Attorney. Bertrand Witherspoon was a lawyer. It made sense. Someone on the board could have leaked the story, someone who believed, as Mom did, that the museum shouldn't be keeping it a secret. All I knew was it wasn't me. Don't misunderstand me—it's not like I wouldn't have leaked it if I'd had the chance. I just didn't have the chance. Like I would know who to contact at the Sunpapers anyway.

Connie grumpily finished her breakfast and grouched at me again, whereupon Mom told her not to be so surly with me.

Maybe it was because of Connie's sniping, but Mom was in a particularly kind mood as she drove me to school. She asked me if I got tired of packing my lunch and if I'd like money to buy lunch for a change. And she mentioned taking me shopping soon for some new blue jeans, something I'd been bugging her about for awhile.

Now, any time a parent is really nice to you, your antennae go up, sensing trouble, and I was no exception. As Mom maneuvered the car through morning traffic and maneuvered the conversation around all the wonderful things she was going to do for me, the question that kept echoing in the back of my mind was: "Why?" Why was she so focused on my feelings all of a sudden? My hair was looking good, so there was no more need to sympathize in that regard. Did she know something I didn't know? Was I failing? Was she going to ask me to give up my room, or tell me I had to quit school and go to work to put Tony through college?

Shortly before we drove up to the high school, the bombshell dropped.

"There are plenty of boys out there, Bianca, and you'll find the right one. If you ever want to talk about it, I'm here."

What?!!!! She was slowing down in front of the long walkway that led to the school's front door. I knew she wouldn't want to linger because of traffic, but this could not go unresolved.

"Doug and I are . . . well . . ." I started to say.

"I know. I saw him with Kerrie downtown last week. But you'll find someone else. Like I told you, plenty of fish in the sea. And you can still go to the Mistletoe Dance—with one of your friends. That's what I love about dances nowadays. You don't have to have a date. In my day, if the boy didn't ask you, you were left sitting at home."

Crash. That was the sound of my heart hitting the concrete sidewalk and breaking into a thousand pieces. Kerrie and Doug downtown? Kerrie and Doug together— maybe holding hands, or his arm around her shoulder, or in some position that told my mother we were "kaput" and they were "in like Flint"—whatever that means.

What a way to start my day! After I slammed the door shut, I practically ran up the sidewalk to the school, fighting back tears. When your mother notices your boyfriend might not be true—that's really, really bad news.

Inside, I raced to my locker and hurried through the morning routine. I didn't linger to see if Sarah or Kerrie or Doug showed up. I wanted to be alone. In fact, I was so into this alone business that I skipped lunch, just eating an apple in the hallway, and went to the library instead. Let them all wonder where I was. Let them miss me. I felt like kicking pigeons.

For all my efforts, I was rewarded by a few confused looks from Doug as we passed in the hall during the day, no reaction from Kerrie (I hardly saw her), and at least some concern from Sarah, who caught up with me after school.

"Hey," she said as she wriggled into her fleece jacket. It had turned a little chilly over the weekend as a cool front moved through. "Something the matter? You looked kind of down today."

I had to use every ounce of self-control not to burden Sarah with my Doug-and-Kerrie story. I so wanted to tell her. I wanted to sob it all out, to rant at the sky and gnash my teeth and rend my garments. My best friend and my boyfriend! This wasn't fair. This broke all the rules!

But I had my own rules. I knew if I complained about Kerrie stealing Doug, it would only add fuel to the dry tinder of Kerrie and Sarah's relationship. I didn't want to go there. So instead, I used all my effort and pasted a smile on my face.

"Nothing. Just thinking about the case—the art case, that is."

"Did you see the article in today's paper?" Sarah asked, her eyes widening. "I'm so glad they didn't mention Hector."

"Yeah, me, too. That reminds me—I was thinking that maybe there's a connection between the alarm going off and this whole thing."

"You mean the day you were with me at the museum?" Sarah asked.

Wow, did that day ever seem light years away. We had been planning a surprise party for Kerrie, something we hadn't talked about since.

"Yeah. I was maybe thinking that whoever is doing this wants attention and they thought pulling the alarm would get it. But it didn't, so he had to leak the story to the paper when the museum started covering stuff up."

Sarah grimaced. "Fawn Dexter is going to be in a bad mood today."

Usually, the pre-Christmas days are really happy ones for me. I still haven't lost that holiday glow from childhood, where you look forward to what Santa is going to bring. Even knowing there's no Santa hadn't really dimmed my joy. But man, oh man, this season I was feeling like a regular grinch. With all the troubles swirling around my friends and my love life, I could barely focus on school work, let alone shopping. So when Neville called after dinner that night to invite me to a holiday party at his place, my first reaction had been to say I thought I would be busy. When he pressed me, I reluctantly said I'd call him later and tell him for sure what my plans were.

"You have to go," Connie said, standing in my doorway. Obviously, she'd overheard.

"Since when are you my social secretary?" I replied with all the warmth of an Antarctic traveler.

"Since Bertrand told me Neville is lonely and trying to fit in!" She leaned against the door. "I met with him today. And I'm on retainer."

"Bertrand? Does Kurt know about how cozy you've become with Bertrand?"

Connie gave me a look that said, if she'd had a pillow with her, she would have thrown it at me. We Balduccis have perfected silent communication to a high art.

"Besides," I continued, "didn't you and Neville have a hot date? Don't you think he'd want you there instead of me?"

"Bianca!" Connie groaned. "Come on. You know that if he were just some guy, completely unconnected to anything I was doing, you'd feel sorry for him and go to his party. You'd probably be starting some Befriend-the-Brit program at school." Her voice softened. "You know that's true."

She had a point. Even with Neville's slightly obnoxious personality, chances were that Kerrie and Sarah and I would have taken pity on him and tried to bring him into the fold of normalcy. Just because doing so would help my sister was no reason not to go to his party.

No, there was another reason not to go—and that was because of Neville's interest in me when I had a boyfriend—if I still had a boyfriend, that is.

"The problem," I said gently, "is that Neville likes me. And I don't like him—not in that way, at least."

"Neville likes everyone!" Connie said. "And he had this mistaken idea that American women like men to be forward."

"What?"

"He tried to lock lips with me after the concert," Connie explained, "but I told him 'whoa,' and the rest of the night he was the perfect gentleman."

"He *what?*" Her suggestion was that, in Neville's eyes, I wasn't some special hot tamale he couldn't keep his hands off. I was just an ordinary tamale.

"He apologized and told me he thought I'd expected it—thought all American girls did." Connie laughed. "Frankly, I think that was just a line of you-know-what, but he was friendly afterward, so I think he tries to see how far he can go, and backs off when you set limits." She crossed her arms over her chest. "In other words, sex kitten, if you make it clear you have a guy, he won't bother you."

"Oh," I said, searching for some funny and sassy retort to throw at her. But my mind was too jarred by her ego-bursting story. Here I'd thought Neville hit on me because I was such a babe in my new haircut and all. From the corner of my eyes, I glanced in the mirror over my dresser. Hey—I *was* a babe. I wasn't relinquishing the title just because Neville had thrown me back into the pond.

"Well, maybe I'll go," I said at last.

"Great! You can get Doug to take you. That'll send everybody a message." Her job done, she waltzed off down the hall.

I looked at the phone in the middle of my bed. Hmm . . . ask Doug to a party at Neville's. What kind of message would that send? Well, it could send a message of cavalier insouciance (I've always wanted to use that word in a sentence!), of a sense that I didn't care about Neville, and that I was so sure of my love for Doug I could go to a party at Neville's and take Doug with me. And if Doug was hooking up with Kerrie, it would force him to 'fess up, and at least I'd know where I stood.

On the other hand . . . it could send a message of complete disregard for Doug's feelings if he thought I was interested in Neville, and Doug was still interested in me. What's a girl to do?

The phone rang, jolting me by surprise. Wow—I ask a mental question and the phone rings. This was, like, weird.

When I picked up the receiver, the weirdness continued. It was Kerrie and she was calling about Neville's party!

"Sarah and I are going," she said after the hello's, the exchanges about schoolwork, snarky teachers, and new clothes. "And Doug said he was interested. C'mon, we can go as a group. It'll be fun."

Doug said he was interested? My "boyfriend" told Kerrie he was interested in going to a party before he told me? Was I going to go now?

Heck, yes.

"It's kind of spur-of-the-moment," I said, pretending not to care. "I mean, I'd have to get Connie to drive me—"

"Doug said he'd drive," Kerrie said, irritating me even more. "He said he could pick you up at 6:30."

"Okay," I managed to mumble, and then I let Kerrie chitchat with me for another fifteen minutes, finally using the excuse I had homework to do to get off the phone and mope. I was in Mopus Extremis, and felt like a big dark cloud was pressing down on me.

Chapter Seventeen

Nothing much happened in the days leading up to Neville's party. In fact, we entered a kind of eye-of-the-hurricane period where you just knew the worst of the storm is creeping up on you, but you let yourself believe sunshine and blue skies are here to stay.

Doug was still acting strange, hardly talking to me, and even avoiding eye contact when we passed in the hall. Now, ordinarily I'd have thought those were really bad signs, even portents of doom, if you know what I mean. But I was in serious denial. After all, we had this date thing coming up—the party. Okay, it was more a "semi-date" since we were going as a group. But I had my pride and I insisted on thinking of it as a date.

In fact, I invested quite a bit of time pondering what to wear for this date. I decided I needed to really impress on Doug that I was still his girl, still worth having as a girlfriend, and still worthy of his trust. Okay, okay—if he was dumping me for Kerrie, I wanted him to suffer with yearning.

So I pawed through the darker recesses of my closet and in no time at all found the perfect party outfit.

Actually, it took me about two hours to find it. I did a

lot of try-ons, standing in front of my mirror in a broom-stick skirt (too hippie), new jeans (too casual), sundress (too beachy), short black dress again (too obvious), and even khaki shorts and flamin' crop top (too trashy, and besides, too cold for early December).

No, what I decided to go with is a look I think of as "sleek but sweet." I found a pair of pinstripe pants I'd forgotten I had—maybe I should clean up the closet more often—and paired them with a stretchy red top with three—quarter sleeves and gathered bustline. Since the pants are also snug, they both brought out my best feature—I'm slim. I can eat virtually anything and not gain a pound. I've got some supercharged metabolism that burns up calories before they even get to my mouth. It drives Kerrie nuts, but she's got curves where I've got angles, and with the Doug thing going on, I wasn't feeling too sympathetic.

Anyway, in this number, I looked tall and thin and so-phisticated and hot, but also not too flashy.

The night of the party, I paired the outfit with a simple gold chain with my birthstone on it—a garnet—and with matching earrings my mom gave me one year. With my hair brushed and my body perfumed, I was ready.

First problem—the pickup. Doug was late. He didn't pull up to the door until nearly 7:00, when I was ready to either start calling emergency rooms or put out a con-tract on his life. And to make matters worse, when he came up to my door, he didn't apologize. He laughed!

"Ready?" he said between chuckles.

"Uh-huh. What's so funny?" We walked down the steps to the car, which he'd pulled into a parking spot. Well, "pulled into" is too generous a phrase. The car stuck out at a forty-five degree angle, with its rear bumper halfway in the street.

"Kerrie. She was just telling me about Baker's music history class." He shook his head at the memory, obviously still enjoying her scintillating conversation.

"Yeah, I have him for chorus," I said, trying to get in on the fun. When we got to the car, I noticed Kerrie was in the front seat. Uh-oh. Another bad sign. But she immediately jumped out to let me in, big smile plastered on her face.

"No, that's okay," I said to her, getting in the back. Okay, so I wanted Doug to protest. But he didn't. Instead, after we were all buckled in, he told Kerrie to regale me with her humorous anecdotes about Baker. I felt like punching them both.

And when she did tell me the story, I was miffed. I already knew about the "Amazing Grace" trick. I'd hoped to tell Doug that one myself but had forgotten.

Oh well, at least that anger distracted me from my other bad feelings. Like envy. The envy I felt when we arrived at Neville's and I noticed for the first time what Kerrie was wearing. A short denim skirt, beige sweater and . . . boots! How could I compete with knee-high boots, for crying out loud?

Luckily for me, she disappeared into the crowd almost immediately after we arrived, or I would have had to rip them off her.

Neville's house was more like a palace. It was in the northern part of the city, a kind of privileged class zone, behind a brick wall and wrought-iron gate. It had a Tudor-style look to it with big jutting wings and tall windows and even a curved turret-like thing stuck on one corner. Oh, and from what I could make out, the lawn looked landscaped. Not just mowed and clipped. Landscaped. As in "put the delphinium over there, Jeeves, and the Siberian irises by the fountain." This was serious money.

Neville greeted us with a big smile and a glass in one hand. He was drinking. Uh-oh. I don't drink and neither do any of my friends. Sure, we know kids who do. But I decided long ago (okay, okay, maybe just when I entered high school) that I wasn't going to bring that kind of sorrow to my mother's door.

"Do come in!" Neville said and made a big sweeping gesture to the inside of the house. A big gesture that ended up sloshing beer on me. Yup, that's right. Beer on my perfect outfit. Beer my mother was sure to smell on me later. Good grief.

Neville didn't even notice. Someone called his name and he was off into the house before I had a chance to say "get me out of here quick." And then Kerrie was summoned by someone she knew and the party hit full tilt.

"I've got to get this out," I said, pointing to the spot on my slacks where the beer had sloshed.

"It won't show," Doug said. He kind of had to shout because at that moment someone had turned up the volume on the CD player big-time and some rap singer was shouting out lyrics right next to my ear. At least that's the way it sounded to me.

"But it smells!" I walked off down the entrance hall searching for the kitchen. Darn Doug. He didn't show any sympathy for my beer spill, but he'd been all over Kerrie after the sushi avalanche at the art museum.

Neville's house was big and confusing. To the right of the entrance hall was a huge living room where a fireplace glowed and several couples were engaged in serious make-out sessions on various sofas. To the left was another huge expanse—a dining area of some sort with furniture that looked like it belonged in a museum. Beyond these rooms was a staircase, a bathroom, a guest room, a work-out room, and a family room that had so much electronic equipment in it that it could have doubled as a Circuit City showroom.

Finally, finally, just across from this room—where the party was going full swing—I found the kitchen. In there, a nice maid helped me dab the beer from my pants. That's right. A maid. Neville sure was raising the bar as far as parties went.

"Thanks," I said to the woman.

She just smiled at me, and turned back to a tray of dip and chips—I mean "crisps"—that she was getting ready. When I went back into the hallway, Doug was nowhere to be found. The music was blaring, but I heard laughter coming from the family room, so I tried there. About a dozen kids were laughing and talking. Some of them, like Neville, were drinking. I only recognized one or two of the people, and wondered where Neville came up with the rest of this crew. Kerrie was talking in the corner to a girl I didn't know, and Sarah, who'd arrived before us, was chatting with Hector. Hmm . . . Neville must have invited everyone he'd met since arriving in the New World.

I went back into the hallway and looked up the stairs. Oh, what the hey. Maybe Doug was checking out the rest of the house. I walked up the steps, which curved around to the second floor. The walls were decorated with art, and I noticed right away that some of it looked exactly like the abstract expressionism at the museum. In fact, one of the paintings looked strikingly similar to the Bargenstahler we'd found in Sarah's trunk! My heart pounding, I walked on into the dim hallway.

Although I'd started this search to find Doug, now I

was on a different mission. I wanted to see if I could detect a pattern. Bargenstahler. Maybe he had more of them. I looked into a room to the right at the top of the stairs. Nothing. Just a bathroom. All right, a pretty spectacular bathroom, with gold spigots and warm brown marble, but a bathroom nonetheless. Beyond this, a bedroom, clean as a whistle, looking unlived-in. Probably a guest bedroom. Beyond this an office. I stepped inside. It was dim, with only the milky light from the moon illuminating everything in shades of charcoal and gray. Peering into the darkness, I let my eyes adjust to the light. On the walls were some paintings, but I couldn't quite make them out.

Flick. Lights. Action. Caught! Someone had turned on the lights. Startled, I jumped and looked at the doorway. Neville. He leaned against the jamb.

"Nice, huh?" He nodded to the paintings.

Now that the light was on, I had a chance to really look them over. They were landscapes. Beautiful, romantic landscapes. Rolling hills in autumn. Spring ponds. Summer ocean. Not at all like the Bargenstahler or the other art works on the staircase wall.

"Who did them?" I asked after swallowing hard.

Neville shrugged and came closer. He squinted at the signature. "Oh . . . Mummy! I forgot she'd painted these."

"Where *is* your mother?" I asked.

"Mummy and father have been divorced for some time. She's an art dealer in London. Thought I mentioned that." He hiccupped.

An art dealer who also painted? I remembered his theory—that the thief could be someone trying to make a point.

"Has your mother been to America recently?" I squeaked out. Yup, that was subtle.

Neville laughed. "No, she's too busy to travel. Keeps saying she'll take holiday when business slows down."

"Does she paint a lot?"

"Not an awful lot. Come here, I'll show you some more." He led me down the hallway to the next room I had intended to explore. It was obviously Neville's room and it was as messy as the other ones had been neat. In fact, it reminded me of my room, except maybe kicked up a notch value-wise. Where my room was dollar-store style, Neville's was brand-spanking-new-expensive-designer-label style. A big four-poster bed jutted out from the far wall, its rich green bedding mussed and a few pairs of trousers strewn at the end. A desk cluttered with papers and a Hopkins catalog sat under the window. Cherry dresser and nightstand completed the bedroom suite, and a massive armoire was pushed against the wall opposite the bed. Its doors open, it showcased a TV, DVD player, stereo, and other equipment I didn't even recognize. When Neville saw me staring, he chuckled.

"Don't know what half that stuff is. Can't even program the damned time into the thing." He pointed to a flashing timer, then turned to the wall by the bed, and nodded. "Here you go. These are of the countryside around our home."

Along the wall were four small paintings, exquisitely rendered, of lush valleys and distant hills. They had the quality of photographs, but were enlivened by a deeper sense of feeling—something a lens couldn't capture. I was impressed. And my mouth hanging open probably communicated that oh-so-elegantly to Neville.

"Poor Mum. Can't find a market for her stuff amongst the la-de-dah crowd." His voice, so cheerful a moment ago, now sounded sad.

I looked over at Neville. He wasn't smiling any more.

His lips were shut tight and his brows furrowed. Was he trying to make a point? I shook my head. No, not Neville. It couldn't be! After all, he was the one who'd originally suggested the art-thief-as-message-sender theory.

"How long have you been in Baltimore?" I asked.

"Oh, let me see now . . ." He scratched his head, "Since the summer. Oh, but before then, I came over to scope things out. In the spring. Why?" His sunny mood came back and he walked over to me and put his arm around me to gaze at the paintings. Although it made me uncomfortable, I let him keep it there. I wanted to keep him talking.

"Does it bother you that your mother's work doesn't sell?"

"Hmm . . . I don't know. I suppose. She's very talented. One doesn't like to see any talent go to waste, no matter who the poor soul is." He didn't sound very passionate on that score, but maybe he was covering.

"So she doesn't paint much any more?"

"No, too busy, like I said."

"But she'd paint more if she was selling?"

"Why, yes, I suppose she would." He laughed, then turned to me and put both his hands on my shoulders. "That's well sweet of you, Bianca, to ask so many questions about Mummy. Why, one might even think you were interested in me." And then he did the kissing thing again! He swooped in on me and planted a light warm smooch on my tender lips. I was about to explain that no, I wasn't interested in him, at least not in that way, but he was a fine "bloke" all the same . . . when my boyfriend did it for me.

Yup. Doug chose that moment to play caring companion. He stood in the doorway, and with his mouth hanging open and his fists clenched by his side, I almost expected him to say something like "take your hands off her this instant, pardner, or I'll have to blow them off with this six-shooter of mine." Instead, he said nothing and walked out of the room.

And I ran after him. "Doug! Wait! You've got it all wrong!"

He increased his pace, and I chased him down the staircase and out onto the lawn until I finally caught up with him by the babbling fountain.

"Look, where are you going?" I said at last.

"Nowhere. Home. I don't know." He shoved his hands in his pockets and stared at the ground.

"You can't go home. Not without me and Kerrie. You're our ride."

"Sarah can take you."

"I don't want Sarah to take me. I want you to."

"Didn't look that way to me."

"I told you—nothing was going on. Let me explain!" And then I told him about my little investigative foray into the upper floors, and how Neville liked to think of himself as a lady's man, and how I was about to tell Neville to stop when Doug had shown up on the scene.

At first, Doug didn't say anything. Then he grimaced. Then he looked back at the house. And I was ready to scream at him. Just say it! Say you don't care! Hurl more accusations! Just say *something!*

Okay, if he wouldn't do it, I'd do it for him.

"You don't believe me," I said softly. "And you don't because you know Neville already kissed me once before." I told him that story, too, and how Connie had had the same experience.

"It's not me, Doug. It's him. He's kind of a ladies' man. Or thinks he is. He doesn't mean any harm. He's kind of desperate, don't you think? I mean, who are all these people at this party?"

"People he's met," Doug volunteered. "Some of them just recently."

"See what I mean? He's lonely. He's trying just a little too hard. At everything."

That did the trick. When I sidled up to Doug, he put his arm around me and even kissed me on the top of my head. But now that I had him in sympathetic mode, I decided it was time for me to hurl the accusations at him. Didn't want the opportunity to go to waste. So I spilled out my own little bag of resentments about how much time and attention he'd been paying to Kerrie lately. I expected a protest and maybe even an argument, and instead got laughter.

"It's nothing, let me tell you. I just thought you'd be upset if Kerrie was upset. And so I was trying to be nice to your friend."

"You mean you don't like Kerrie?"

"I like Kerrie," he said, "but she's not my kind of girl."

"She *is* kind of high-maintenance."

"I'll say."

And then he hugged me tight and all was right with the world.

Chapter Eighteen

We didn't stay at the party much longer. Too many people we didn't know. Too noisy. Too much booze. So I was home well before my curfew but with a far lighter heart. Doug even went out of his way and took Kerrie home first so he and I could share some private moments together on my doorstep before calling it a night.

I was in such a good mood, in fact, that it didn't even bother me that someone had rearranged the poetry magnets yet again. Now, they read:

> *Life dreams big and bold*
> *Grab action, sister*
> *Friend flirt totally wild*

All right. My bet was on Connie now. "Grab action, sister" seemed like her style.

In the morning, I was ready to tackle a whole new world, and part of that was continuing to plan Kerrie's birthday party. Now that I knew nothing was up with her and Doug, I could throw myself into that activity full throttle. I started by calling Sarah and asking if she wanted to get together. She said "yes" right away and we made plans to meet at the Enoch Pratt Free Library downtown, ostensibly to go over a "project."

There was another reason I wanted to talk with her, though. As I'd fallen asleep the night before, I kept hearing Neville's voice as he talked to me about his mother's art. It had been so different—so sad and serious and lonely. Not at all like the chipper Mr. British-Stud voice he used most of the time. It bothered him big-time that his mother wasn't getting anywhere with her stuff. And if it bothered him enough, maybe he could be the culprit. The fact that he was the one who came up with the theory of the caper as an act of art vengeance fit in with that. If he was nuts enough to pull this off, he was nuts enough to draw attention to it, to brag about it.

Anyway, I wanted to talk to Sarah about this—see if she observed anything I missed at Neville's house—and get more info out of her about Hector to help clear his name. Time was running out. I knew my sister, and I knew she'd be making a report to the museum soon. And now that the whole thing had been in the papers, the police were going to get involved. Not good for Hector if he was still the main suspect.

I had Tony drop me off in front of the big box-like library building and looked down Cathedral Street for Sarah. Within a few minutes, her battered blue car came slowly into view. Unlike Doug, she was pretty good at parallel parking and had her car into a metered spot with a few easy turns.

"Hey!" she said when she got out.

"I have a lot to tell you," I said as she walked over to me. Before we were even in the front door, I'd spilled the beans about Neville, his mother's art, and my theory. Okay, so it was his theory, but I was telling it, and possession is nine-tenths of the law. Or something like that.

Sarah was a happy camper when she heard my ideas. She said Hector was getting pretty depressed about the whole thing and was thinking of leaving town.

"But that'll make him look even more guilty," I said.

"I know," she responded. "I keep telling him to hang on."

I sighed and twisted my mouth to one side as I thought. "I keep thinking about the security tapes," I told her. "The problem is Hector had access to them. And somebody switched them."

"Well, other people probably had access to them, too!" Sarah sounded frustrated. She put her keys in her pocket and rocked on her heels. "Fawn has keys to everything. So do a bunch of folks in the museum."

"Fawn . . . Neville said his dad and Fawn were cozy," I mused. "Maybe Neville got the keys that way. Have you ever seen him hanging around the office?"

Sarah stared into the sky and did the scrunched-up mouth routine. "No . . . but that doesn't mean he wouldn't have had access. I overheard her making plans to go out with Neville's dad last week. And I know that Neville's been checking out Hopkins, which is just around the corner from the museum. And I've seen her keys sitting out on the desk more than once. It would be pretty easy to grab them . . ."

"Have they ever been missing? Do you know if she's ever complained about losing them?"

"I don't know," Sarah said, her voice getting high and excited. "But I can find out. I can ask her this week."

"Okay, that's a good start. If we find out her keys went missing at some point, we know Neville had a chance to grab them when he was there with his dad."

With that settled, we headed for the library to make other plans.

"Oh, darn," Sarah said before we went in. "Forgot my notebook—it's got all the ideas I wrote down for the party. And my notes for my project. It's in the car."

I waited for her at the door, but when she got to her car, she didn't grab the notebook. Instead, she waved me over.

"What?" I asked, rubbing my arms. It was getting colder and I was wearing only a sweater. No way would I wear that fashion mistake parka again—even if I was on the North Pole.

"Neville! I just saw him go by."

Uh-oh. First Hector, now Neville. I didn't even need to ask. I hopped into the car as Sarah slid behind the wheel and turned on the engine.

"Get in!" She was already putting the car into gear as I closed my door and started buckling my seat belt.

"Where are we going?" I asked.

"Following him!" She pointed straight ahead. Neville was driving his father's big silver Mercedes.

"He'll see us," I said, remembering Connie's previous instructions about needing two cars to do a good surveillance on wheels.

"Nuh-uh. Wait and see." Sarah let Neville take off down the road. When he was turning onto Mulberry, she took off, not at racing speed, but at a good clip all the same. But it didn't take long before Neville turned—a wide left onto Charles that almost put him into the left lane facing oncoming traffic. Boy, he still hadn't gotten used to this driving on the right thing.

Sarah didn't follow right behind him. Instead, she ducked onto a small street, Hamilton, then wove back onto Charles, then back again. I was getting seasick from all the turns. But darn if she wasn't good at this—far better than Connie, who was supposed to be the professional. After several loops and turnbacks, it was clear where Neville was headed—toward the museum!

"Are you thinking what I'm thinking?" I blurted out.

"Yup." She pressed down on the accelerator and zipped up and over to St. Martin's Drive, looping behind the Hopkins campus. We couldn't see Neville's car any longer, but since we were both sure we knew where he was headed, it didn't matter.

And sure enough, when we did get to the museum, his car was parked in the lot with no Neville to be seen. Sarah made sure we were out of sight, parking her distinctive blue Olds two blocks from the museum.

"Let me go see what's happening," I volunteered.

"Not without me!" She undid her seat belt at the same time I did, and we exited the car together. First, we walked casually up to the broad steps to the front of the museum. There we stopped. To go farther meant traversing an open sidewalk. If Neville returned, he would see us. There were a few Saturday museum-goers around, but not enough to constitute a crowd in which we could get lost.

"Come on. Let's make a run for it." Sarah rushed out into the open, sprinting past the steps. I followed, huffing and puffing when we reached the other side.

"Have you considered going out for track and field?" I said between gulps of breath.

"Shh . . . There he is." From our hiding place behind some shrubs, she pointed. Neville was coming out of the museum. And in his hand was a flat, dark parcel—just the kind of thing you'd put a painting in. To make matters even more conclusive, he was hurrying, looking both right and left as if afraid of being spotted. The museum parking lot was crowded. Perfect—snatch something when lots of people are around, when guards are keeping an eye on shady-looking folks. Not folks like Neville, a son of a board member, well-dressed, polite . . .

Okay, I admit it—I was excited. We had him red-handed. Hector was off scot-free now. All we needed to do was get the police involved.

"He's leaving," Sarah whispered.

"We should call the police," I said. "Or at least Connie."

"Don't have a phone, do you?" asked Sarah.

"Nope." We're a one-cell family, not counting Connie's business cell phone. And Mom had the Balducci mobile.

"Besides," Sarah said, "we don't know what he has. Come on. We've to get back to the car." As soon as we were sure Neville was in his vehicle and not looking, we did the sprint routine again, retracing our steps back to Sarah's car. In a few seconds, we were on the road again, this time headed toward Charles going north, several blocks behind Neville's car. It was starting to rain, a soft cold drizzle that blurred the windshield. Sarah's wipers didn't do too great a job, either, and they made such a horrible racket I was afraid Neville would look back to see what all the noise was about.

At 39th Street, Neville turned right, heading into the confines of Guilford. He was headed home.

"Maybe we *should* just pull over and call the police now," Sarah said, biting her lower lip.

"No, you were right before," I said, my brain cells kicking into gear. "We don't know for sure what he has. We have to unmask him ourselves. Come on. Just a little while longer."

Sarah followed at a discreet distance until we turned into a dark, shaded drive. Uh-oh. A private drive. Neville's drive. Up ahead, Neville's car disappeared behind lush evergreens. Sarah slowed to a snail's pace. As we rounded a curve, we saw his house, big and mansion-like, its black-shuttered windows looking like closed eyes.

"No farther." Sarah stopped and put the car into reverse. "We'll go back to the street and do the rest of this on foot." Looking over her shoulder, she backed the car up the drive.

And backed it. And backed it. Until she came to the wrought iron gate.

Yup. A wrought iron gate. It had been open—obviously—when we followed Neville in. Now it was closed. Must have been one of those automatic gates, and Neville had pushed the button to close it once he was home. We both stared at it in panic.

"What do we do now?" I whispered, as if Neville could hear us.

Speaking of Neville . . .

"Hullo, ladies, nice of you to visit!" He stood, umbrella in hand, right outside my window.

I shrieked. Sarah jumped off her seat.

"Didn't mean to startle you. Come in, come in. Just having a spot of tea. Join me, why don't you?" Neville gestured to the house and I looked at Sarah. She shrugged and we both got out.

To stay under the umbrella, we leaned into either side of Neville, and we walked to the huge house like the three stooges.

"Perfect timing, too," he said with good cheer. "I just bought my father the sweetest gift and I want to show it to you—a signed print! Just picked it up at the museum gift shop! You can tell me what you think."

Chapter Nineteen

Despite the fact that tailing Neville turned up diddly, I wasn't ready to scratch him off the suspect list. If anything, our little visit with him made me even more convinced he was the one. During tea-time with him, I asked him more about his mother. He opened up a lot about her and talked virtually nonstop about how talented she was, what kinds of art she handled—abstract expressionism!—and how awfully hard she worked. He told us her birthday was coming up and he was going to go shopping the next day for something really "grand." Not only that, he revealed that he was lonely for home and was thinking of talking to his father about letting him go back to London! Sarah and I exchanged a couple of wide-eyed looks that clearly communicated the following:

Are you thinking what I'm thinking?

Oh yeah. This guy would go to any lengths to help his mother.

And vamoose out of town after the misdeed is done.

After Sarah and I managed to escape the Witherspoon estate, she dropped me home just in time for dinner. Mom cooks on the weekend, and I don't like to miss her terrific meals. I managed to come in the door just as she was putting chicken and dumplings on the table—real dumplings she made herself.

I pretty much snarfed down my meal in silence. It was just Mom, Connie, and me because Tony was working. And since Connie was always quiet on Saturday nights—probably because that's when she felt the need to have her own place the most—dinner conversation once again consisted solely of sentences that began with "Pass the . . ."

That was until the end, when Mom pushed back her chair and looked at us both with the "Tasking Eye," which is the look she gets when she's about to tell us to do something.

"You're up," she said looking at each of us. "And the dishwasher hasn't been unloaded yet." With that, she left the room.

I looked at Connie. "I'll load if you do pots and pans."

"Then you're unloading, too."

"That goes with pots and pans."

"Nope. Dishwasher duty is dishwasher duty."

She got up to leave. "Call me when you're done."

"Connie! Wait a minute!" I stood and started scraping plates. "I want to tell you a few things I found out about Neville today."

That did the trick. She lingered by the door.

"Probably nothing I don't already know," she said.

"Oh, really? Like the fact that Neville's father has a Bargenstahler in his home here?" I went to the dishwasher and opened the door. "Oh dear. This will take me so long to do." I looked up at her, all sweetness and light. "But if I had help, then I could tell you more quickly what I know."

Connie snorted. "You can tell me while you work."

"Nuh-uh. Want to focus on the dishes first."

Connie looked at her watch. She probably had a date. With a groan, she trudged to the dishwasher and began unloading it.

"Okay, give. And it better be good."

So I told her about the night at Neville's party, about the paintings, about Neville's "Mummy" and her failed art career, and about following Neville earlier that day. I timed the whole story perfectly, too, so that the last syllable was tumbling from my mouth just when Connie was placing the last tumbler in the cabinets.

"That's odd." She twisted her mouth to one side. "Bertrand never mentioned anything to me about his wife. Or, for that matter, about owning a Bargenstahler."

"When were you talking to him?" Now that the dishwasher was empty, I began to do the loading routine.

"Just yesterday. I had a meeting to go over what the firm expects of contractors, etc." She crossed her arms over her chest. "And we talked about the museum case. I specifically mentioned the Bargenstahler."

"Not the stuff about one possibly being in Sarah's car!"

"No, not that. I was just talking about how that kind of art was difficult to appreciate. And he agreed with me."

"Maybe he was being polite."

"No. He was pretty fired up about it. He even quoted Tom Stoppard to me. Said 'modern art is imagination without skill.' It was like a little art lecture."

"Yeah, but still . . . he could just be showing off how much he knows and all."

"I guess. But he sits on the museum's board, for crying out loud. I thought it was a little odd at the time, but now . . ." She glanced at the clock above the sink. "Look, I gotta run. Thanks!"

And before I'd even had a chance to tell her how

Sarah was going to snoop around Fawn Dexter to find out if her keys had ever been missing at work, Connie was off to DateLand.

I didn't realize what a juicy tidbit I'd provided my sister until the next day, when she offered to go Christmas shopping with me after church.

You have to understand—Connie wouldn't offer to do something like that unless she was feeling really grateful or sympathetic. So she must have really appreciated my scoop on the Witherspoon household and hoped to get a little more. We headed for the mall around noon.

And you know what? We actually had a good time. Sometimes it works out that way with siblings—they're fun to be around. We picked out a gift for Mom—a gift certificate at Hecht's. Yeah, it sounds pretty boring, but when I look back at all the gifts I've given Mom over the years, I cringe with embarrassment—a huge artificial orchid pin (that she actually wore to church one Sunday), an exercise video, a fuzzy key chain, bright orange gloves, and a silk scarf that looked like it had been an awning in a previous life. Nope, she'd get a lot of use out of a gift certificate, especially if Connie and I pooled our money. (Tony was on his own.)

And with Connie's help, I also managed to find a gift for Doug that I think struck the right tone. Since Doug will be doing the college-search routine before long, I bought him a "College Survival Guide" and a pair of really cool leather driving gloves. Even if he isn't a cool driver, he can at least look like one, right?

So I was feeling pretty happy and organized when we decided to head to the Food Court for a snack.

When we sat down, Connie started asking me more about the case, and even asked me for my opinion! I was in heaven. That summer job was looking more and more like a real possibility. So, I again went over everything I had learned, thinking of even more details from my afternoon with Neville.

"The only problem is, we can't figure out how Neville would have gotten the keys to the room holding the security tapes," I said. "Sarah's going to ask Fawn if her keys were missing recently."

"They were," Connie said. "I already asked a bunch of administrators. Fawn misplaced her keys a couple weeks ago and had to have duplicates made."

A shiver went through me. It suddenly hit me—I could actually be right. It happened so rarely that it felt, well, cosmic.

"Did the keys ever turn up?"

Connie nodded over her straw, sipping at her double mocha chocolate espresso cappuccino ice. "Yes. They were in her desk drawer, right where she left them."

"Except they weren't there when she was looking for them," I said, stating the obvious.

"Right."

"But how could Neville—I mean, was he at the museum a lot?"

"From what I can tell, he and his dad are together a lot. He could easily have pocketed the keys when he was there with Bertrand." Connie smiled at me. "You know, you might have solved this case, Bianca."

Wow. Did I hear that right? Had my sister just told me I had solved one of her cases? I gulped and spluttered.

Well, not really. But I did get a goofy grin on my face.

"What do you do now?" I asked.

"I'll check out the keys stuff and see when Neville was around. I'll look into his mother's background a little more. Into Neville's—"

All of a sudden, I remembered something Neville had said. "He might be leaving town," I blurted. "He said he's lonely."

Connie's smiled faded. "Crap. That means we have to hurry this up."

"Aren't the police involved?"

"They're moving a bit slowly—playing catch-up."

"This pretty much clears Hector, though, don't you think?"

"It could."

We lapsed into happy silence, and I was about to ask Connie if she could call Fawn that afternoon to find out about Neville's presence at the museum, when I looked over and saw—Neville himself!

He was sitting alone at a table, with a big brown shopping bag—the kind with rope handles. He *had* said he was going to go shopping for a birthday gift for his mother, and this mall was the best place to do that.

But he looked kind of . . . funny. *Funny* as in weird. He wasn't eating or drinking anything. He was just kind of staring at his hands and frowning, with this pasty look on his face like he was going to be sick. In fact, my first thought was that he had a hangover.

"Look, there's Neville," I said to Connie.

She turned and looked to where I'd gestured.

"Maybe you should go say hi."

"What!?" Now that Neville was *the* suspect, I was suddenly afraid to talk to him.

"Well, if you want to do this Private Eye thing, you have to gather information. You could talk to him about visiting the museum with his father."

Okay, that was enough for me. After all, my goal was to get a job with Connie during the summer. As far as I was concerned, this was an "assignment," or at the very least a test of my skills. I looked longingly at my drink, took a quick sip for courage, and headed Neville's way.

He was so absorbed in his thoughts that he didn't even notice me until I was right on top of him. And instead of his usual sloppy come-on grin, he looked startled, even unhappy that I'd stopped by.

"What are you shopping for?" I asked, pointing to his bag.

He grabbed at it and closed it tightly. "Nothing! Nothing! I mean, I'm returning something. Didn't fit. A shirt. That's all." Then, as if he realized just how lame that sounded—after all, that was an awfully big bag for a single shirt, and he'd told me already he was going to search out a gift for his mother—he switched on his charming light and smiled from ear to ear. "How about you?"

"Christmas shopping with my sister." I gestured toward Connie, who waggled her hands in the air when she saw us look her way.

"Oh, I see."

I hadn't known Neville all that long, but I did know that the normal thing for him to say at that point was "why don't you join me?" Or at least a "want to do something together?" After all, we already knew the guy was lonely and desperately trying to make friends.

Instead of those offers, however, he remained nervously silent, even biting his bottom lip and tapping his fingers on the table. "You know, I really must be off. Forgot I was supposed to meet my father. Awfully nice to run into you." He stood, grabbed his bag, and left.

When I went back to Connie and explained the conversation to her, she didn't say anything at first.

"A shirt, huh?" she eventually asked. "I don't think so."

"Are you thinking what I'm thinking?" I said, even though I wasn't even sure what I was thinking, only that Neville was hiding something.

"Yup. C'mon!" She stood, took a final, caffeine-jolting gulp of her drink, and tossed the empty cup into a nearby trash can. "We're going to follow him."

"Not again!" I clambered after her, juggling my drink with my purse and bags.

"What *again?* We never followed Neville before." She took long strides toward the door.

"Maybe you didn't," I muttered, but she didn't hear me.

Following Neville this time was tricky business. The parking lot at the mall has a crazy layout, and sometimes we've had trouble finding where our own car was parked, let alone following another car. But we were in luck. Neville was getting into his dad's Mercedes just a couple rows over from where Connie had parked her car. We walked a few rows out of the way, though, so he wouldn't see us.

I'd barely gotten into the car before Connie was taking off.

"This'll be tricky," she said, slowing down. "Not many cars around and I don't want him to notice us." She reached behind her, pulled a white canvas beach hat out, and scrunched it on her head. "Duck."

"What?"

"Duck down. Or slouch. Or something. At the very least, we can try to make ourselves unrecognizable." She placed sunglasses on her face to add to her new beach-comber look. Meanwhile, I slid down in my seat.

"Don't you have another hat?"

"I don't know . . . Look in the backseat!"

She was turning left and right in quick succession as she wove through the parking garage, so searching

Finding the Forger

through the debris in her backseat was like trying to find a life preserver while the ship was pitching to and fro. Not good for the stomach. Especially one that was now home to a double chocolate mocha espresso cappuccino ice. Ugh.

All I found was a hideous straw thing with plastic flowers on it and a chiffon bow tie for under the chin.

"Yeah, wear that," Connie said.

"Are you nuts?" I said. I put the hat on my lap and just stared at it. For all I knew, it was alive and could hurt me. "Where'd you get this thing?"

"Secondhand shop. It was going to be a gift for you." Connie veered out onto York Road and headed south. "Put it on!"

I did as she said, but hated it. "A gift for me? You *are* nuts! Or maybe just unusually cruel!"

"It was going to be a gag gift, silly. Don't worry, I already picked out a real gift." She slammed on the brakes at a red light, and my flowered hat nearly flew off my head, which would have been okay with me.

I put on sunglasses, too, so no one would recognize me. To heck with Neville. I didn't want *anyone* I knew to see me in this getup.

"He's getting away from us!" As soon as the light turned green, Connie took off down the road, quickly turning right to find a back street that paralleled York Road, and checking at each intersection to see if she could find Neville's car in the traffic. He was heading into town, and there weren't many places there he could be going.

"I'm thinking the museum. What do you think?" she asked me.

"Uh . . . I think so," I said, even though I had no idea where he was headed.

Libby Sternberg

"Yup. The museum. He's probably headed there."

I didn't feel this was the right time to tell her that Sarah and I had already done this follow-Neville-to-the-museum-and-home routine. I'd left out the details of that trip when I'd given her my Neville information. It didn't matter. Connie was intently staring at the road.

She eased off the accelerator and turned back to York Road. She was going to let him get ahead of her and meet him at the museum. Okay, I'd go along for this ride.

"Poor Neville," I said, suddenly feeling sorry for the guy.

"Yeah, it's sad. Kid's caught in the middle of a divorce. Mother's trying to get ahead in the art world but isn't doing the stuff that's in vogue right now. Kid's shipped off to Dad. Kid decides to make parents enter a world of hurt, and what better way than this? Embarrass Daddy on his home turf. Show Mommy how much he loves her . . ."

"You're freaking me out here, Connie. You sound like a psychiatrist or something."

She shrugged. "It's not complicated. Just common sense."

Before long, we were at the museum, which wasn't open yet for visitors. But there, alone in the parking lot, was Neville's father's car. And Neville was just sitting behind the wheel, staring at his hands as if he didn't know what to do.

It was oddly disappointing and kind of anti-climatic, if you know what I mean. I'd expected a long chase and some melodramatics. Maybe even a race on foot around the museum grounds. Instead, Neville just sat there, as if he were waiting for us—or someone—to come along and stop him before he stole again.

Before I could say "boo," Connie veered into a spot behind him and was out of the car. I followed her, completely forgetting I had that kooky hat on. Funny thing about hats—you forget you have them on while they're on, but you feel like you have them on once you take them off. Go figure.

"Neville!" Connie shouted.

Neville looked up, and his face was ghostly white, stricken, as if he were coming to grips with some painful event. He rolled down the window.

"What are you doing here?" he asked quietly.

"I think you know." Connie stood next to his car and I stood right behind her. What a pair we made—she in her beach headgear, me in my clown outfit. "What's in the bag, Neville? It's not a shirt, is it?"

His mouth fell open, and it looked for an instant like he would protest. Then his eyes widened as if he realized all was lost. "No, it's not," he said slowly. "I . . . I . . ." He hung his head in shame. Then he pulled the bag from the passenger seat and handed it to Connie. She carefully pulled out the bag's contents—an abstract expressionist painting about the size of a calendar, with bold clean lines done in reds and grays.

"Can I talk to my father first—before you do anything?" he asked. He sounded so pathetic, you could hardly say no. Connie handed him her cell phone.

"How do you work this thing?" he asked softly.

Chapter Twenty

In retrospect, giving Neville the cell phone may have been a mistake. It meant Neville's dad came swooping in before the police got there, refused to let the cops talk to the kid, and whisked him away before I even had a chance to say good-bye, let alone remove that darn hat from my head. Just my luck, too, that a Sunpapers photographer showed up with the men in blue. They snapped a photo of the scene, including me in the floral contraption. Connie had wised up and removed her headgear by then.

It was a sad story, though, and I can't say that I feel really proud of myself. In fact, I think all of us—Kerrie, Sarah, and Doug—had a case of the guilts after it came out. Connie had pretty much gotten the story right. Neville was really troubled by his parents' divorce, had even been seeing a therapist for awhile, and had come to America specifically to see if he could snap himself out of a depression and start over. His father and he hadn't always gotten along. He adored his mother . . . it was practically a textbook case.

But once we heard it, we all wished we'd reached out more to him beyond the superficial "isn't he the cutest thing" stuff. And in Doug's case, he wished he'd made an effort beyond the "get your hands off my girlfriend, ugh ugh" stuff. Doug had even imitated Neville a couple times in the last week, and been pretty darn good at it, too.

But all that quickly evaporated into the past because, just two days after Neville's arrest, he was gone—as in out of the country. His father must have arranged it, even though Bertrand Witherspoon said he had nothing to do with it. And his mother, contacted in London, wasn't sure where Neville was even though she didn't sound all that worried in the television interview I saw.

To make up for all this trauma, Mom took me shopping on Tuesday night and let me buy a burgundy velvet dress that screamed "oh yeah, baby." Meanwhile, she promised to finish the green dress for Christmas.

The only cloud on this horizon was that it was too late for Mistletoe Dance tickets. So Kerrie, Sarah, Doug, Hector, and I decided to make a special night of it by going out to dinner on the last day of school before the holiday break.

And you know what? With Neville taken care of, Doug and I back together, and Kerrie and Sarah friends again, I wasn't too upset about not having tickets to the Mistletoe Dance. Sure it was the biggest dance outside of the prom. And it was a holiday dance, which meant it would be particularly festive, with mistletoe and everything. And it would be the only dance where you could wear a totally cool winter dress . . . Wait a minute, maybe I *was* upset!

I pushed those feelings aside as I powdered my nose and glided on some lip gloss. The usual holiday hits were blaring from my clock radio. Focus on the good stuff, I kept thinking—it wasn't too bad going out to a posh restaurant with Doug and my friends. Giving him his Christmas gift. Getting mine from him. And no Neville around to mess things up.

But the thought of Neville brought the black cloud of nagging sadness into my room.

"What time is Doug picking you up?" my mother called from the hallway.

"In a half hour. Why?"

"I want to take pictures."

Since she couldn't see me, I rolled my eyes. "Okay!"

Standing, I looked at myself in the mirror and felt pretty darn good, even though I was just in my slip. This haircut looked even better, now that the just-cut edges had mellowed out a bit. It was a keeper. After dabbing perfume behind my ears, I was just about to shimmy into my dress when my mother knocked on my door.

"Connie's on the phone for you!"

Opening the door a crack, I grabbed the cordless from her outstretched hand. "I didn't even hear it ring!"

Mom just shrugged. "Turn your radio down."

"Hello?" I said into the phone.

"Bianca? I can hardly hear you. Turn your radio off!" Connie's melodious voice shouted at me through the receiver. I did as she said.

"Why are you calling? I've got to get ready to go out."

"This'll take just a minute. Can you go in my room and get my Witherspoon file?"

Groaning, I pulled on my robe and walked to her room. "Why didn't you have Mom do this?"

"I figure you've already snooped in the file, so I'm not breaking any confidentiality with you. Why involve Mom?" she snickered.

"Where are you, anyway?" I opened her bedroom

door and flipped on the light. She didn't need to tell me where the files were. Without being directed, I headed to the standing file on the corner table by the window.

"His office at his home. Witherspoon's."

"You forgot to take his file with you?" I plucked it from the bunch, and for once it was easy to suppress the temptation to look at the other files stuck there. I needed to get going. My little burgundy dress awaiteth.

"I grabbed the wrong one. No big deal. I just need to check on one thing. Open to the expense account information. It should be in the back. I need to tell him . . ." She chuckled and I heard a bell-like noise followed by a whir and music. "His office is phenomenal. Tons of electronics. You should see this clock he has."

"Huh?" Flipping through the pages, I found the ones she was looking for. "Got 'em. What do you need? And why are you meeting with him, anyway? I thought you were off the payroll once you turned his son in."

"He's leaving his firm. Going to London to meet with his ex about Neville. Then taking early retirement. I thought he might leave a recommendation for me with someone else at the firm."

"That sounds like a long shot."

"Well, yeah. But I've got to make a living."

"What do you need? I've got the file, but I've to get going."

"The total. It should be at the bottom of the page. It should be the expenses plus retainer."

As I rattled off different figures in response to her questions, she interspersed our conversation with more awe-struck comments about Mr. Witherspoon's at-home electronics. Just as we finished, her tone changed and she started talking to someone else, telling him she was describing his office to me, her sister, because it was so "dazzling." *Dazzling?* Was that supposed to impress him? I held the phone away from my ear and silently gagged. Then I heard Witherspoon speak. "Yes, I'm a gadget aficionado. I think I should have been an engineer." Connie came back on to say thanks, she had to go.

After I replaced the phone in its hall cradle, I went back to my preparations, which didn't take long. But I was distracted. Something nagged at me I couldn't quite figure out. After attaching my fake diamond chip earrings to my ears, I shook my head to try and knock the feeling out of me, and went downstairs.

In a few minutes, Doug came in and Mom did the "ooh, aah" routine and snapped some pictures. Even Tony poked his head out of his room and his silence was as close to a "you look great" pronouncement as I'd ever get from him, so I was a pretty happy camper.

The beginning of the date went well, with Doug giving me a goose-bump-inducing kiss in the car before we took off. This was going to be a great night.

Next stop was Kerrie and Sarah's, where we did the ol' picture-taking routine again. As I waited in the Daniels' foyer with Doug, the nagging feeling came back. What was it? Connie calling me for help. That had to be it. Something out of the ordinary. Something that didn't fit.

No, it wasn't that. It was something else that didn't fit. What was it? What did she say? He said he'd wished he'd been an engineer.

An engineer. Someone who was good with electronic things. Someone who could fix a VCR/DVD so it wouldn't blink. Someone who could tape shows in a flash. Not someone like Neville, who didn't know all the functions on his cell phone!

"You look nice, Bianca," said a smiling Mrs. Daniels. Kerrie came into the room and frowned.

"Where's Dad?" Kerrie said. "We have to get going. Sarah and Hector are already at the restaurant."

"He's on a business call. He'll be right down." Mrs. Daniels walked upstairs to get her husband. In a few minutes, he was downstairs snapping pictures, and we were all going through the "ooh aah" routine all over again.

On to the restaurant, and still I couldn't shake it—something not fitting. Why should it matter if old Witherspoon had wanted to be an engineer? And there was something else now—Mr. Daniels on the phone, his business phone.

But I couldn't think about those things because we were starting our festive dinner with a gift exchange. I was thrilled to get a book I'd been wanting from Kerrie, and a bunch of body sprays and nail polish from Sarah. They were both pretty pleased with my gifts of scarves and earrings. And Doug was genuinely happy with his riding gloves, which he tried on right away.

But man, oh man, did he take the cake! He gave me a little velvet-covered box, and in it was—a locket! An oval locket in shiny gold. And inside were two goofy pictures of us we'd had taken at one of those machines at the mall one Saturday.

"Doug!" I looked him in the eye and squeezed his arm. "This is beautiful!"

"Let me help you put it on." He took it from me, stood behind me, and attached the clasp.

"Kerrie," I said, suddenly teary-eyed. "You knew. You helped him pick it out."

"Hey, at least he thought to ask for help!"

"Yeah, I do get some credit," Doug laughed.

"We almost didn't think he'd be able to get it," Kerrie said. She picked up her menu and looked at it again. "I'd seen it at that antique jewelry store, and they were getting ready to close . . ."

"So I called them," Doug said. "And then I called Kerrie to make sure it was the right one."

"Yeah, and then we had to convince the guy to hold it for him. I think he wanted to jack up the price!" Kerrie laughed.

So that was probably when my mother had seen Doug and Kerrie together—when they were shopping downtown for my gift. What a crazy couple of weeks this had been!

Sarah rubbed her head like she had a headache.

"I should have driven," Hector said, looking at her with concerned eyes.

When we all looked at them with question marks on our faces, Sarah explained.

"My trunk is still broken," she said. "Because of that, Hector thinks the exhaust leaks into the car and gives me a headache."

"He could be right about that—get it fixed," Doug said seriously.

"I'm taking it to a mechanic tomorrow."

I remembered the night we'd opened up Sarah's trunk and found the painting—a painting that had yet to turn up, by the way. Maybe that was what was bothering me—that incident. The painting there one minute, and gone the next. Someone who had known where she was had to have taken it. And the only one who'd known where she'd gone that night was Hector because he was the only one to call her at the Daniels's house.

Wait a minute. Hector had called Sarah on the Daniels' home phone. There was another phone in the house. The business phone.

"Kerrie," I said with sudden urgency. "Do you remember the night Hector called looking for Sarah—the Sunday we went to the museum opening? The Sunday when I spilled sushi all over you?

Kerrie looked at me like I had two heads. "Yeah."

"Did anybody else call—on the business phone—that night?"

She pulled back as if I had crazy cooties she might catch if she got too close. "Yeah. I remember because my mother wanted Dad to watch a PBS show with her that night and he waved me into his office and told me to tell Mom he'd be right down, he was on the phone with Bertrand Witherspoon."

My heart was thumping fast. Bertrand Witherspoon. He knew electronic gadgets. He knew how to switch the videotape on the security cameras. He had access to the museum. He knew art! And Connie was talking to him right now, finalizing her account with him.

"Call your dad!" I practically shouted at Kerrie.

"What?"

The waitress came over and set our appetizers before us.

"Call your dad and ask him. Did Mr. Witherspoon ask him about Sarah that night?"

At the mention of her name, Sarah peered at me suspiciously. "What are you thinking, Bianca?"

"There's no time to lose. I'll explain later." I asked Doug for his cell and dialed Connie's number while Kerrie dialed her dad. You know all those people who get really annoyed when they see folks talking on cell phones in restaurants? They would have had an outragefest if they'd seen us.

"Connie?" I asked when she came on the line. "Don't talk. Just listen."

After she quietly gave me a fake cheery hello, I rushed in with my explanations. "Witherspoon's the one. He's the thief, not Neville. And my guess is he's not going to London. He's probably going to vamoose to some country where he can't be extradited."

"Uh . . ." she mumbled.

"Look, I'm putting all the pieces together now—" At that moment, Kerrie looked at me with wide eyes and nodded her head, whispering that Bertrand had called her dad on the night in question and had asked about Sarah. "—but here's what I need you to do. You have to stall him. Keep him from leaving while I call the police and—"

Just then Bertrand Witherspoon's booming voice came over the phone. "That won't be necessary, Miss Balducci. Calling the police, that is."

Connie's voice came next, dripping with disgust. "He was showing me how to hook up my cell phone to the speaker phone system when you called, you numbskull!" That's what I love about Connie—the way she effortlessly lays on the guilt trip, even under duress. Now I'd placed her in jeopardy, a fact that was confirmed by Bertrand Witherspoon's next icy words.

"You call the police and you'll never see your sister again, Miss Balducci. You've now turned me into a desperate man willing to do desperate things."

I gulped and could hardly speak. I must have looked like a ghost because Doug and Kerrie started asking me what was the matter. I shushed them with a waving hand, and pressed the phone hard into my ear as if that would bring me closer to a solution.

"Look, Mr. Witherspoon," I said, loud enough so the others could hear me, "I didn't mean to mess things up for you. I just wanted to solve the mystery, you know. Ask Connie—she and I have some competitive thing going on here. Right, Connie?"

"Uh-huh," I heard her say. Her voice was a little high-pitched, which hit me in the gut because it meant she was a little afraid. For all I knew, Bertrand Witherspoon had some kind of weapon trained on her.

"I don't really care about any wacky new art at the museum," I continued. "For all I care, they could burn all that stuff and no one would be the worse for it."

Hector cringed when I said this, but I plowed forward anyway. While I talked, I blinked my eyes at Kerrie, which in Balducci-In-Jeopardy language meant "Call your father! Help!"

"It was all a game to me, sir. Just like it was to you. Just an innocent game." While I talked, I saw Kerrie picking up her cell phone again and dialing. With Sarah and Hector behind her, she stepped away from the table to make the call in private.

"Get up!" Witherspoon said, and I knew he wasn't talking to me.

"What are you doing?!" I practically shouted.

At that point, our waitress came over and asked if something was wrong with the food that none of us was touching.

"Who is that?" Witherspoon asked. "Where are you?"

"Home! I'm home." That was . . . our maid. Lucinda!" Holding the phone away from me, I said, "Thanks, Lucinda. That will be all," and I couldn't help saying it in some phony baloney accent. What was the matter with me, anyway?

Witherspoon snorted. "I'm leaving," he said into the phone. "This particular game is over."

No, he couldn't leave! He had Connie! Who knew what he'd do to her now that he knew the jig was up! My hands were slippery from sweat, my face was hot

181

from blush, and my heart was pounding so fast and loud I was sure Bertrand Witherspoon's high-tech gizmos were recording it *and* my blood pressure over the line.

"Don't leave! Neville's here!"

At first there was silence. "Neville's—" he started to say, then stopped. I had him. "Neville left. I know. I took him to the airport."

"He came back!" I said. "He's here right now! He's downstairs. Let me go get him for you." Relieved to have the break, I put my hand over the mouthpiece in a death grip and looked at Doug. "We've got to get out of here."

Immediately, Doug pulled out his wallet and threw some cash on the table. Sarah and crew followed suit. The waitress, meanwhile, rushed over.

"Is anything—"

"Family emergency," Doug said, putting his arm around me.

Once outside in the brisk evening air, I ran to the car with Doug right beside me. "Get in and turn on the radio loud," I said in a hush. A few seconds later, he was in the car with the music blaring. Then and only then did I take my hand off the mouthpiece.

"Neville! Neville! Someone's on the phone for you. Your father." I raised my eyebrows at Doug, who was behind the wheel, and I held the phone out near the door. And Doug—my Doug, my sweet, bright, funny Doug—knew exactly what I wanted and stepped up to the plate.

"Not on your life!" It was his best-ever Neville imitation, and the times he'd done it just to irritate me melted into the night. And then he threw in a curse, just as he'd heard Neville curse, and through the music and the distance, I knew he would sound just like Neville, even to Neville's dad.

In fact, if there is an aural equivalent of a drained face, Mr. Witherspoon's voice as it came over the phone next would have qualified for the blue ribbon.

"What?! Let me talk to him! How'd he—Put him on the phone right now!"

"He won't talk to you, Mr. Witherspoon," I said. At the same time, I gestured to Doug to start the engine. As it roared to life and we stepped into the car, slamming doors, I covered the mouthpiece again.

"What was that? Where'd you go? What are you trying to pull? Remember, I have your sister." And then I heard him moving as if they were leaving the room together. Connie!

"Don't you dare hurt her, Mr. Witherspoon." Why was I calling this creep Mr. Witherspoon as if he deserved respect? He had my sister, for crying out loud. "I'll . . . I'll . . ."

Doug turned a corner sharply and the phone fell out of my hands onto the car's floor. Since when did Doug drive over the speed of a snail's pace? As I glanced at him, I saw a new look on his face, or maybe I just hadn't noticed it before—determination and courage. He was heading toward the Witherspoon home. I hadn't even had to tell him.

When I picked up the phone, I was heartsick. I'd lost the connection. Would he let Connie answer if I called again? What was I going to do? Tears pooled in my eyes. What could I do to stop Witherspoon? And stop him from doing what? Was he so desperate that, to get away, he'd actually harm Connie? Of course he was. He'd let his only son take the fall for his misdeeds. The man was capable of anything. My stomach turned. I thought I would be sick.

"Has somebody called the police?" I asked, miserably.

"My dad did," Kerrie said. "What happened? Did Mr. Witherspoon hang up?"

"I don't know . . . I don't know what to do. I don't know . . ." I mumbled, afraid of crying in front of my friends.

"Call him back!" Doug said forcefully. "C'mon. Don't let him win. Call him back!"

"What will I say? I don't know what'll stop him."

"He thinks you're with Neville," Sarah said quietly. "You could use that."

"He doesn't care about Neville!" I practically shouted. "He let him get pinned with the art theft. What kind of father would do that?"

"He didn't exactly let him get pinned," Sarah said again.

"That's right," Kerrie said. "Neville pinned himself. He probably figured it out and didn't want his dad to go to prison, so he took the fall for him. Then his dad bailed him out by giving him the money to get out of the country."

Hector snorted. "Right. Some family!"

"Tell him you're going to turn Neville in. Tell him Neville came back because he's in love with you," Doug said.

"All right. I'm going to try again. I want you all to talk like there's a party going on, okay?" They solemnly nodded their heads and I turned up the radio. Then I punched in Connie's cell number.

They had to be the longest ten seconds of my life, waiting for her—or someone—to answer. While the phone rang, I imagined all sorts of awful scenarios, ranging from . . . well, I don't even want to think about them. But finally, finally, just before it would have kicked over to voice mail, he answered the phone.

"What do you want?" This time he didn't sound so self-assured. And his voice echoed. He'd moved to another spot.

"I dropped the phone, Bertrand. No need to worry." I was in control. I could feel it. He was afraid, and I knew exactly what he was afraid of. Kerrie, Hector, and Sarah were doing the party routine in the backseat, chatting it up and laughing, while Doug had the radio turned up so high I could hardly hear. It didn't matter. That's exactly the effect I was after. "You're going to have to speak up, Bertie," I yelled. "We've got a real party going here. Lots of 'birds,' as Neville would say." Then I half-covered the mouthpiece, knowing Witherspoon would still be able to hear. "Hey, Nev, leave her alone—she's my best friend!"

As if on cue, Doug piped up in his Neville voice. "Oh, bugger that," he said. I could have kissed him.

"He came back because he's in love with me, Bertie. And you know what? I'm not in love with him. So I was just about to call the cops . . ."

"What do you want?" Witherspoon's voice sounded almost frantic now.

"Let me talk to Connie." When he hesitated, I continued, laying on the table precisely what I knew he didn't want to hear. "You put her on the phone by the time I count to ten or I'm going to get off this phone and dial the police. I know people there, Bertie. I won't have to go through some screening process. I say the word and someone's at your place in a flash. One, two . . ."

"Bianca?" When Connie's voice came on the phone, I could have cried with relief. She sounded nervous, but not too afraid. She even sounded a little amused. She was probably trying to figure out just what kind of game I was playing.

"Are you all right, Con?"

"Yeah, fine."

I didn't want to say too much because I was afraid Witherspoon would be able to hear. No telling what kind of gizmos he was capable of hooking up. For all I knew, he had an earphone set plugged into the phone and was listening in on every word we said.

"Neville's here," I lied. I knew Connie would know it was a lie. "We're having a party." If she didn't know I was lying before, she would surely know now. "He just showed up on our doorstep. Didn't go away after all." Now I was hoping Witherspoon *was* listening.

"I told you he didn't," she said smugly. I could have punched her for trying to sound like she knew more than me.

In reality, I could have hugged her for being so self-confident around a maniac.

"I told you he liked you too much," she continued. Through the noise and confusion in the car, I could hear Witherspoon's breath. As I'd suspected, he was on the line. "He told me that the day of the reception."

The day of the reception? Connie had been nowhere near Neville that day. Besides, Neville and I had just met— hardly enough time to form a Krazy-glue bond.

Witherspoon spoke up. "All right, listen up," he said with more confidence. "We'll make a deal. You bring Neville to Martin's Airfield. You know where that is?"

"Yes," I lied. Someone would know where it was. Plus, I wasn't sure that's where they were anyway.

"I'll have your sister there, and we'll just exchange her for Neville."

My heart, which had calmed down to a mid-Indy 500

pace, was now zooming at finish-line speed. Something wasn't right. I couldn't trust him. But I let him keep talking.

"You come around to the back of the airport and tell the guard you're with me. A private jet will be there waiting. I'll let your sister out as soon as I see Neville is safe. And if you bring anyone else with you, the deal is off." He clicked off the phone.

As I closed the flip phone, Doug turned the radio down and my friends stopped their noisy chatter. My party-in-a-car stopped while the car itself moved steadily forward.

"What's going on?" Doug asked almost at the same time Kerrie asked, "What are we going to do?"

"Your dad is getting the police to go to his house, right?" I said, half to myself and half to Kerrie and the rest of them.

"Yup."

"That's where he started, but he said to meet him at Martin's Airfield," I said slowly.

"You don't sound like you believe him," Sarah interjected.

"Doug, you want me to drive?" Hector asked. "I know where Martin's is."

Although Doug was going faster than his usual turtle's pace, he was still being careful not to speed.

Doug shook his head no.

"Witherspoon's voice sounded strange—echoey," I said, peering out the window, feeling scared silly. "Someone call the police. Tell them to head to Martin's."

"The lobby of his office building—maybe he was there," Sarah offered. She leaned forward and grabbed the back of Doug's seat. Kerrie got on her phone.

"No, not enough time to get from his home to his office in between the first and second call," I said. Wherever he was, we had to figure it out soon. "Connie was trying to tell me something."

"What did she say?" Hector asked.

"She said Neville told her he liked me at the reception."

"The exhibit opening reception?" Sarah asked. "Maybe he's got her somewhere Japanese. It was a Japanese print exhibit. Or a print shop! Does he own a print shop?"

"The museum," Doug said and deftly turned the car onto Charles Street to head in that direction. "That's where he is."

"Yes! That's it!" I could have jumped up and down. "It was echoey, like the museum. And Connie was trying to tell me that's where they were because the reception was there and . . ."

"And it's only a few minutes from his house!" Kerrie said. She pulled out her cell phone again and I knew she was going to dial the police one more time.

"No, don't!" I told her and leaned back to put my hand on the phone so she wouldn't punch in the numbers. "I don't want to alert him to the fact that we know."

I looked at Sarah and Hector. "Tell me where he could be in the museum. Where would he take her?"

Now it was Hector's turn to lean forward. "He's probably going to put her in the storage room in the old wing and lock her there. No one checks that room. She'd be there all weekend."

"Do you have a key?" I asked.

With a huge grin, he pulled out his key ring, which was full of keys. "He'll leave her there, then call you when he's safely away," Hector continued.

We were now turning into the Hopkins campus onto

the drive that led to the museum. It loomed behind trees in the dark and I felt like I was going to be sick.

"Bianca," Hector said softly as if afraid Witherspoon could hear us. "You must call the police and tell them. You can't do this on your own. We can't do it on our own."

Slowly, I nodded my head and punched in the number while Kerrie called her dad. By the time the explanations were over, Doug had pulled the car into a parking spot a block from the museum. We all sat silently in the car for a few minutes, nobody saying anything as we waited.

"I can't stand this!" I said at last. "What if he hurts her? We're all assuming he won't, but he's a desperate man! What if Neville calls him while we're waiting here and Witherspoon finds out we've been lying? He'd do something . . ." I choked up and Doug put his arm around me.

So we got out of the car and crept up to the museum. Hector used his key to let us in. As soon as we crossed the threshold, I felt a chill. It was spooky in there. With only the security lights on, creepy shadows made fearful images on the walls and floor. We stood silently, waiting to hear something.

And it didn't take long. From upstairs, far away, we heard the dull thud of a door closing.

"Come on," Hector whispered and we all followed him up the stairs on our tiptoes. But once we got up there, the need for speed got the better of me and I ended up rushing through the sculpture gallery at such a pace that my heels made a muted clip-clop on the marble floor.

Suddenly, a voice called out from the darkness up ahead.

"Who's that?" It was Bertrand Witherspoon, and he sounded even more desperate than before.

I turned to Hector, Doug, and the rest. "You guys hide," I whispered. "Let me take care of this."

"No way," said Doug, and my heart melted again. But I was too intense for too much sentiment, so I shook my head.

"Uh-uh. He was talking with me on the phone. I'll deal with him. You guys stand behind those pillars until I give you a signal or something."

Without a word, they disappeared.

"It's me, Bianca!" I called out into the blackness. "I came to get Connie."

"Where's Neville?"

"He's in the car."

"I told you to take him to the airfield."

"Hey, I might not be the class valedictorian, Bertie, but I'm no dummy. I knew you weren't there."

"All right, then. Go get him."

"Not so fast, buster. I want to see my sister."

There was a pause, and I knew either one of two things was going on. He either didn't have her—had locked her in a closet as Hector had speculated—or he was wondering whether bringing her out would be a good move. I held my breath, only letting it out when he spoke again.

"I want to see Neville first." But I heard a soft sneeze coming from his direction. Connie's sneeze. Good ol' Connie.

"Look, Bertie. The jig is up. Soon, a hundred different cops are going to be swarming all over this place. Either they take you or they take Neville. Which is it going to be?"

"You lied to me!"

"C'mon, Bertie. They're gonna be here any second now. They see Neville sitting alone in that parking lot, and they're all over him like white on rice. Give up Connie and you can go grab Neville before they arrive. You're wasting time, Bertie. You could be on your way . . ."

I heard a soft grunt and a splat like someone falling, and for a second my heart jumped into my stomach because I thought maybe he'd—I don't even want to say what I thought. But before I could go too far down that heartbreak road, I saw Connie running toward me from out of the shadows.

Toward me and right into me, to be precise. We both toppled to the floor in a painful heap.

"Hey!" I said.

"I couldn't see you in the dark!" she said.

It didn't matter. I was so glad to see her, even her shadow, that I could have hugged her. But I restrained myself. In the distance, we heard Witherspoon's footsteps.

"Let's follow him!" I said to Connie after we'd righted ourselves.

"Bianca! What's going on?" Sarah whispered from behind a pillar.

"It's okay! Connie's safe. You can come out!" In a second, the whole crew was out and I was leading the charge toward where Bertrand Witherspoon had disappeared.

"He parked near the dumpster!" Connie said.

"But he'll head to the parking lot—he thinks Neville is there," I said.

We clomped and clicked our way downstairs. It's amazing the noise even the softest shoe makes in an echoey museum with marble floors and walls. As we sprinted toward the doors, it sounded like the racetrack at Pimlico.

Too late. Bertrand Witherspoon was outside, looking bewilderingly at an array of flashing blue and red lights. For a second, I almost felt sorry for him. He'd been looking forward to seeing his son, and instead he was met by a sea of cops. My sympathy lasted about an eighth of a second, though. Bertrand Witherspoon was a jerk of the first order.

I learned something that night—I love my sister. Imagine that!

Actually, I learned more than that. Remember how I said this was a story about false assumptions? Boy, was it ever! First, everyone assumed Hector was the culprit because of his background and, let's face it, his ethnicity, which was probably a factor, too. Even I thought he was a good suspect from the get-go without so much as a smidgeon of solid supporting evidence.

And then, when Hector was cleared, and Neville was cornered, we all nodded our heads sagely. Of course it was him, we all smugly thought. If not the poor Latino with a record, then surely the obnoxious Brit with an attitude problem. Who would have thought it was his father—upstanding, no record, congenial, well-liked? Yet, underneath it all, he was a roiling sea of resentment, and, according to Kerrie, with money problems to boot.

He had Neville's upcoming college bills to pay, and his bank account had been cleaned out because of some poor investments. But no one knew, least of all his family. He was "keeping up appearances," fooling everyone, including himself.

He'd tried to sell off some of his art and found out it wasn't worth much. And at a meeting of the museum board, some folks got to talking about how publicity, good or bad, really jacks up the price of pieces by these new artists—just as Hector had explained to Sarah. So Witherspoon had hatched an idea—steal a painting by one of the artists whose paintings he already owned, and create a public controversy. The papers and TV get the story, and voila! The artist's a hot item. And he can get some good cash for his own little painting. As a private joke, he'd hung, at the museum, a fake painting in place of the one he'd stolen. He thought it would add to the story.

He had a pretty good technique, too. Grab the painting, stick up the fake one, then take the real one to the janitor's bin and throw it in. All he had to do then was grab the painting from the dumpster after the museum trash was dumped in. And, so no one notices, switch the security tapes—security tapes he had access to because he'd stolen Fawn Dexter's keys.

The only time he came close to slipping up was the night of the reception—he'd nabbed a Bargenstahler, replaced it with a fake, and was almost caught when the dumpster was overflowing, and he had no choice but throw the painting into Sarah's trunk. He hadn't known it was Sarah's car, of course—he'd spent a frantic evening trying to figure out whose car it was when he lit on the idea of calling Fawn Dexter to complain about the "old wreck" he'd seen parked by the dumpster at the museum and to ask her if they should have it towed. Fawn revealed its owner, and from there Witherspoon tracked down Sarah to get the painting back.

Poor Witherspoon—he hadn't counted on the fact that the museum wouldn't notice right away that paintings were being replaced. Or on the fact that they'd want to keep the thefts hushed up for awhile. He was the one who ended up "leaking" the story to the press to get attention for the artist.

And poor Neville—he's the one I feel most sorry for. He was just a lonely guy to begin with. Now, he's a lonely guy with a creep for a father. Kerrie and Sarah both told me they'd heard from him, and he still plans on attending Hopkins now that he's been cleared of the crime. But he's pretty shaken up by the whole mess.

As for me, I had one last mystery to solve and that, too, proved to be a case of false assumptions. At breakfast on Sunday, when I complained once again about my poetry magnets being changed, I hit big-time on Connie because it was my way of showing her how much I really loved her.

Mom looked at me like I needed Sanity Pills.

"Why are you screaming at her, Bianca? They're just magnets. I didn't realize they were your magnets! I thought they were fun." So the last person I'd have suspected—my mom—turned out to be the guilty party there, too.

At least I know what else to get her for Christmas this year, in addition to the gift certificate card from Hecht's. In fact, I've already bought and wrapped it—a book of "The World's Most Beloved Poetry," complete with her own set of poetry magnets.

Mari Mancusi

SK8ER BOY

Are you a good girl or a bad girl? Do you allow your parents to micromanage your life so you'll get into the "right college", or do you pierce random body parts (okay, just your belly-button) and hope your parents don't notice? Do you hang out with fashion-obsessed Populars, or do you meet cool new people—like the headmaster's punk-rock daughter Starr? Do you date rich, obnoxious jocks like Brent Baker III—who are so cheesy you can't stomach them without crackers, or do you date an über-hot sk8er boy and fall in love with him—in a tragic, Romeo and Juliet (with text messaging) kind of way?

*Good Girl Dawn Miller is about
to find out just how good it is to be bad!*

- -

Life, Love, and the
Pursuit of Hotties
Katie Maxwell
Author of *The Taming of the Dru*

Subject: Reasons Why My Life Sucks Right Now
From: Emster@seattlegrrl.com
To: Hollyberry@britsahoy.co.uk

1. The end of high school. You'd think that's good,
   right? Not for me.
2. Dorm life. It's going to take forever to hipify all
   those science and techno geeks in the Geek Dorm
   where I'll spend the next four years.
3. Dru's fantasy wedding. If she thinks I'm going to
   wear a pink-and-yellow plaid bridesmaid's dress, she's
   completely wacked out of her gourd.
4. Romantic graduation present cruise...without the
   nummiest boyfriend on the face of the earth? One
   word: *Waaaaaaaaah!*

A Bird, a Bloke, and a Boyfriend

Sally Odgers

A recipe for romance?

Take one bird. (That's Sarah, arm-wrestling champion extraordinaire.)

Add one bloke, who's known the bird forever. (That's A.J., who lives next door.)

Stir in one boyfriend—literally made to order. (That's Clay.) Set the whole thing to rise in a tropical sun-soaked paradise called Pirates' Point, and what have you got?

That depends who you ask. Ask a simple question and you never get a straight answer from anyone....

MY ABNORMAL
LIFE
LEE McCLAIN

"But I'm not normal!"

Fifteen-year-old Rose Graham has never been to school. She's never had a date. She certainly never knew she was gorgeous. She's been too busy shoplifting food, keeping Social Services off her family's case, and taking care of her little sister.

Now, plunged into a foster family in affluent Linden Falls, she's supposed to act normal. But everything seems so trivial when all Rose wants is to get her family back together. At least she has the Altlives computer game to help her cope. And Brian Johnson's broad shoulders to drive her crazy....

Stephie Davis

STUDYING BOYS

HOMEWORK: 0
BOYS: 1

So I study. A lot.

So I have a huge crush on the "wrong guy."

Those two little things justify
my friends blackmailing me?
"Meet some other boys or else...."
Hah. What kind of friends are those?

The kind who can get me grounded.

And get me noticed by that "wrong guy,"
who is actually a jerk and no longer my crush.

Or is he?

Dorchester Publishing Co., Inc.
P.O. Box 6640
Wayne, PA 19087-8640

__5382-9
$5.99 US/$7.99 CAN

Name: _____

Address:_____

City: _____ State: _____ Zip: _____

E-mail:_____

I have enclosed $_____ in payment for the checked book(s).

CHECK OUT OUR WEBSITE! www.smoochya.com
____ Please send me a free catalog.

Didn't want this book to end?

There's more waiting at **www.smoochya.com**:

Win FREE books and makeup!
Read excerpts from other books!
Chat with the authors!
Horoscopes!
Quizzes!